A SHIFT IN THE SKY

IN THE STARS ROMANCE

SUKI SELBORNE

1 CORBY

"Put the weapon down, Ms. Frayne."

"You first."

The leatherclad enforcer and I circle one another, guns pointed squarely in each other's faces. Neither one of us shows any sign of giving up.

"This is a Lazerjet 7TX. Fastest blaster in the galaxy." The enforcer looks down at my thrift store ray gun and smirks. "You don't stand a chance, lady."

I smile mysteriously like I have an amazing secret, and the secret is that my gun is actually way more powerful than his. But I'm bluffing. He's right. My gun's a beat-up piece of shit. I'm just hoping my cockiness will encourage him to walk away.

Enforcers don't like taking risks unnecessarily.

After all, if they had any guts, they'd work *against* the Imperial Order, not *for* it. Like I do.

He sighs sharply. "If you don't drop your weapon, I'll have to shoot you."

"Really? Well okay then, if you *have* to."

He shakes his head, frowning, like he can't quite believe my sarcasm. Can't blame him. Openly defying an enforcer like this really is insane. His firepower way outclasses mine. A single blast from his Lazerjet would atomize me. All I have to bring to this fight is attitude.

Still, attitude has never failed me yet.

He hits some button or touchpad or something, and his gun pulses with a blue glow. Is he trying to intimidate me into backing down?

Then I realize he's scanning me. Good luck with that.

"Nice trick," I say, raising my eyebrows in mock admiration. "What a pretty blue light on your gun. Does it play a little tune too?"

His eyes narrow, and a jolt of adrenaline hits me. For the first time, it feels like there's a real risk of getting shot here. Is he mad enough to hit the trigger after all?

He waits just a second too long before he responds. I take that to mean he doesn't plan to hurt me. Interesting. And it's true, because instead of shooting, he just hits the blue glow button again. Then he smirks at me.

"Yeah. My pretty gun plays the Stars and Stripes every time it blows a guy's head off."

"So cute. And if it blows a *girl's* head off?"

The enforcer is quiet again for a second. There's a high-pitched bleep noise, and he frowns. "Both scans say you're clear." He looks up at me, all the wind knocked out of his sails. "Then where the hell have you stashed the stolen goods?"

"What stolen goods?"

I grin, because we both know I do have something illegal concealed somewhere. But he'd flip if he knew what it was, or where.

Anyway, he's not getting it today. My retina camera transmits footage directly to my probation officer during working hours, and the enforcer will be only too aware of that. He'll have my entire checkered history at his fingertips. And no matter what this dumbass thinks he knows about me, a clear scan means he has to let me walk out of here. That's the law. He can't do a damn thing to stop me.

"Fucking Wildcats," he says under his breath, as he shoves his gun back in his belt holster.

Wildcats is what enforcers call freelance space couriers like me. We're wily and fast, and live on our wits. We're also small-time punks, and no real match for the trueborn members of the Imperial Order. God forbid I ever run into one of those guys. "Neither fish nor flesh," as my grandma used to say.

I can deal with the average human patrol enforcer, no problem. Handling an Imperial Order pure-blood would be way above my pay grade.

If an Imperial Order dude decided a human Wildcat was taking liberties, he'd swat them like a fly. Even if galactic law ordered them otherwise.

The Imperial Order families are all shifters, with patchwork DNA that combines to make them super-strong and super-tall. They're part-human too, believe it or not. But with threads of ancestry drawn from all over the galaxy, they're capable of kicking more ass than the rest of us put together. They're the alphas of this corner of the universe. Luckily they don't really bother with us little people much.

But this guy here? This enforcer is all-human, and pretty low down the food chain, and I thank my lucky stars for that.

"Pleasure talking with you, sir," I say, because the sass never stops. He glares at me, and I saunter back to my ship, whistling.

Once I'm on board, I drop the calm act. I slump into my pilot seat, elbows on the dash, head in hands, panting. My hands are trembling. I feel like I just ran a marathon, in high heels.

"Narrow escape?" my ship's computer Neela asks.

"Yeah."

"Your heart rate is approaching one hundred

sixty beats per minute. Please assume the meditation position."

I obey, because Neela knows her shit. It's actually a relief to hand over responsibility for a few moments. I fold my legs into the lotus position and rest the backs of my hands on my knees. The ship's lighting dims to a soft pink, and the sound of Earth rain surrounds me.

I close my eyes, still and quiet. The sound of the rain is hypnotic, especially when I haven't heard it in so long. The last time my feet touched Earth was months ago. That's because I don't have anything to go back to, since my hometown was razed in the last Milky Way war. Homesickness floods through my stomach, mixed with leftover adrenaline. I feel a little nauseous, and my limbs are tingling, but I know it'll pass.

The scent of lavender drifts across the air. My heart still hammers against my ribcage, but the sense of acute terror is gone already. Neela drops a little birdsong into the soundtrack. I concentrate on steadying my breathing, moving it from shallow and fast to deep and slow. My mind feels tidy again. My nausea fades away completely.

"Your heart rate is now seventy-five beats per minute. Would you like to continue into a full round of meditation, or return to flight mode?"

I fill my lungs with one last hit of lavender-scented air, and exhale. "Back to flight mode, I guess. I need to get off this planet before another enforcer decides to mess with me."

Neela obeys instantly without a word, because robots aren't assholes like me, and the flight deck lights up again. I tap the touchscreen and pull up our coordinates.

"We need to get to Quintagon as soon as possible. I have a contact standing by to take the chip into safekeeping. Can you plot our route, Neela?"

"Indeed I can, commander."

Star charts and cosmic debris forecasts flicker across the screen and disappear again. I use the time to scroll through my messages. A bunch of outstanding payment reminders, a weekly check-in notice from my probation officer, some spam from a company selling holographic vehicle cloaking devices... And a parking ticket for leaving the ship in a no-fly zone on Drancolia. Aw, shit. The last thing I need is an unexpected expense.

"I was only parked for a few minutes," I whine, as I hit Open. What do I have to pay? I scan the message. Seven thousand xenons! Holy shit. There's no way I can afford that.

But if I don't pay, I'll have to stay out of this quadrant altogether. That means I can't work. All the work is here. And I can't come back without having paid the debt. There's no way around it. If my ship gets logged in the quadrant with an unpaid fine, it'll be zapped to ashes before I can say "Who, me?"

Maybe my next job will have to be stealing one of those holographic vehicle cloaking devices, so I can sneak back to this quadrant for business. I'm sure as hell not going to be able to afford one the legal way.

"Commander, we have a problem," Neela says, in her tranquil voice.

I tap my message screen closed. "You're not kidding. Wait, you mean another one? What's up?"

"There's an Imperial Order ship in our path."

"Just fly around it." Those patrol ships are everywhere. They don't care about little nobodies like me. It's not like Neela to bother me with something so trivial.

"Not really possible." She pauses, to ramp up the suspense a little. "It's one of the big ones."

A picture of the ship fills the viewing screen. It looks like a small planet, all by itself. I gape at it. We're on a backwater planet, light years from anywhere significant. This seems all wrong.

"Fuck, Neela," I bluster. "It's a Level A ship. What the hell is that monster doing in this part of the galaxy?"

"I will attempt to find out. Please sit down and fasten your safety belt in the meantime."

I do what I'm told, without taking my eyes off the screen. With a lurch, my ship launches vertically into the air, then darts across the sky at an oblique angle.

"This diagonal flight path is happening for a reason, right?" I shout, as my cheeks flap around from the sheer force of our acceleration. Dignity is impossible.

"We are deliberately launching at an unexpected trajectory, yes. This will allow me to analyse the other ship's response."

My nails dig into the armrests. I can't move my head at all, because we're accelerating so fast. My ship might be old, but she's pretty nimble. At least, if you don't call on her for a speed boost too often.

At last, we burst through the atmosphere into open space. Neela switches off the boosters, and we cruise for a moment.

"So what did the other ship do when we left the area?" I ask.

"It recalibrated its flight path in response to our movement."

I stare at the gigantic ship on the screen. My little ship flying toward a ship of that size is like a bug buzzing around a whale. Put it this way: the Imperial Order ship does not have to move to allow us to pass. Why did it move at all?

"Wait a second, Neela. Recalibrated its flight path? You mean it *responded* to our movement? It's watching us?" I stare at the screen as the truth sinks in. "Where's that ship going now?"

"It's heading right for us," Neela says, her voice as gentle and soothing as ever. "Yes, when we moved, it did too. The ship now appears to be following us."

I swallow, my mouth suddenly dry. Why would a massive ship like that be coming for a little wildcat like me?

The chip.

"They know," I whisper. "Fuck. *They know.*"

I tap the tiny recess in my boot with my other foot, to check it's still there. The chip is safe for now, inside its anti-scanning container. That tiny recess is secret Quintagonian technology that far outstrips anything humans have achieved so far. Even the establishment enforcer couldn't locate the container. It means the chip is almost entirely undetectable.

Almost.

But if I wind up anywhere near Imperial Order shifters, they'll sniff it out in a second.

Pulling my bootlace tighter, I take one more deep calming breath.

"Neela, take any steps you need to take. Fly down a black hole. Hitch a ride on a comet. Anything. I have faith in your ability to find an alternative." The huge ship looms closer on the screen. "Do what you've got to do, Neela. Just get us the hell out of here."

2 JALTON

"You'd better have an ace up your sleeve, Jalton. Or you are *screwed*, little brother."

I concentrate on keeping my face blank. Damn it. My cards are terrible. And I'm rapidly losing the ability to style it out, because it's nearly time to turn them over. Reago's going to beat me yet again. Same as it always was, since we were kids.

I think fast. One last bluff? I never was very good at lying, but I'll give it a shot.

"Let's make this more interesting," I say to Reago. "One more round, and if I beat you..." I think for a second. "I get your personal jetship for a year."

Reago laughs, like this is hilarious. "Sure thing. You're not going to beat me, Jalton. There's no chance of that."

"Try me," I say, stony-faced. That just makes Reago laugh all the more.

"Okay, fine. If you win this hand, you get my jetship." He beams at me, obviously not concerned that this is a possibility. "And what do I get if I win?"

I shrug. "Who cares? You're not going to."

Shit - what's he going to say? My face is hopefully a blank canvas, but my heart sinks to think of the punishment he's likely to inflict. Once an asshole older brother, always an asshole older brother.

"You get his wife-to-be," our friend Kaljo offers. "Lady Simla is mighty fine. A worthy prize."

"Simla has a mind of her own. And she's not my wife-to-be," I say, irritated. "Just because our fathers want the match, doesn't mean it's going to happen."

"Oh, it'll happen," Reago nods. "She's hot. And you're going to obey our father."

I shake my head. Simla *is* beautiful, but I'm not at all interested in dating her. She thinks of nothing but jewels and finery. She has no conversation at all. I find her company dull, even after a single encounter, let alone a whole day. The idea of spending a lifetime in the company of such an empty vessel is dismal.

"So, Reago. If you're not going to steal Simla

away from your baby brother, what are you going to do?" Kaljo asks.

Reago looks down at the table. "I thought of something," he says, with a wicked grin. "A challenge."

I raise my eyebrows at him. "A challenge?"

"If I win, Jalton, you have to do the lowliest job on the entire ship for one day."

I still can't work out what he means, so I stare at him. "Job?"

"The lowliest job. The most demeaning, menial task on this whole ship."

"Like cleaning it?" Kaljo leans forward, looking interested. "You'd give him a *droid's* work to do?"

"No, dummy. The most menial *shifter* job."

"And what would that be?" I yawn, pretending I don't even care because... no, I do care. Because realistically I'm going to be doing it. The bet is unwinnable, with these cards.

"Well, I don't know yet. Kaljo? What's the most menial shifter job on this ship?"

"Prisoner check-in." Kaljo sits back, with a smug smile.

Reago frowns. "Prisoner check-in? Like, what even is that?"

Kaljo chuckles. "You princes need to get out in the real world a little more. We're in charge of the galaxy, right? This isn't just a pleasure cruiser. We patrol the skies in ships like this. We take in prisoners where we find them. Those prisoners have to be checked into the on-board cells, and their own ships are searched by hand. You can't give droids those jobs. They can't tell when humans are lying. So we give the work to shifters. Specifically, to part-human shifters. They're not as sharp as pureblood Imperial Order shifters like us, naturally. But they're sharp enough to sniff out crime and deceit among humankind. And then justice is dispensed according to the crime."

"Oh yeah, Imperial Order shifters can always see when someone's lying." Reago's eyes glitter cruelly at me. "Like you are right now, brother. I know your cards suck. Don't try to hide it any longer."

I start up with a new bluff, but then realize it's pointless. "Okay, fine. You got me." I throw down my terrible cards, face up. Reago and Kaljo guffaw at how bad they are.

Reago lays his own straight flush out with a flourish, and nods. "Well, what do you know? I won. As usual." He shoots Kaljo a wry look. "My baby brother has to do penance. Fifty bars of gold says he's a big failure at prisoner check-in, just like he is at card games. Jalton's too soft for hard work. He's only good for lazy royal life."

Adrenaline surges through me. Reago always knows how to push my buttons. Even though I know he's deliberately provoking me, I react.

"Oh, I'll do your stupid job, Reago. And you'd better hope I don't win next time. You don't want to know what I have planned for you."

Kaljo hoots with laughter. "Down to the cells with you tomorrow then, Jalton. You'll be in your lion form all day, dealing with crooks and killers. Good luck with that."

I slump back in my chair and click my fingers for the serving droid. "Get me another glass of whatever the hell that was."

"Yes sir," the droid replies, and scoots away.

I'm going to drown my sorrows. Tonight is a washout.

So I lost a bet I should never have taken. So I have to go outside my comfort zone and mix with intergalactic lowlife. So what? I could handle it. Tomorrow was going to be long as hell, but I'd live. Probably.

The last thing I remember is convincing Reago and Kaljo to order shots, while singing songs at the tops of our voices. It was a pretty messy night. Lucky I didn't have to get up early for work in the morning, like a regular person.

Oh, shit.

※

I wake with a jump, as a serving droid shrieks in my ear.

"Good morning! Time to awaken, Your Highness. I have brought you a refreshing breakfast drink."

"What the hell?" I mumble, turning over. The clock says it's still the middle of the night, at least to me.

"Would you like me to prepare a fragrant bath for you?"

The droid's singsong voice really pisses me off. I slump back onto the bed, rubbing my eyes. Somewhere inside my skull, a million drummers beat out a painful rhythm.

"Why are you here, droid? Who ordered you to wake me?"

"Prince Reago issued the order, Your Highness. You are expected in the prisoner wing in thirty vilzins' time."

Damn it. Hazy memories of last night crowded back into my aching head.

The bet. I lost a bet. And the payment is... Oh, man. Checking in petty criminals and searching their filthy junkyard-refugee ships. Great.

"The prisoner wing? I don't even know where that is on this ship." Why would I? Royalty never deals with crap like that.

"I can give you directions," the droid says, in her sugar-sweet tone. "Or I can take you there myself. It's up to you."

"Great," I say, forcing myself to sit up. Oh, hell.

The room is spinning. I reach out for my "refreshing breakfast drink", and almost knock it over. Luckily, I steady it just in time. "This drink had better be as refreshing as you say it is," I say, sniffing it dubiously.

"Oh, it is, your highness. It is full of soothing, energizing ingredients and fresh herbs from Quintagon."

"Perfect," I say, and take a sip. It's actually pretty good, although my stomach warns me not to attempt solid food just yet.

How much did I drink last night? It went way beyond my usual level of partying. I'm going to have to grow up sometime, because this irresponsible crap is starting to get old. As old as I feel right now.

"Yeah, please do prepare the bathtub," I say, after a few moments regaining the power of speech. "But don't bother laying out clothes. I have to shift today."

The droid scampers to fulfill my demand, and I put one foot on the floor. Nausea zigzags upward from my belly. I shut my eyes and concentrate on standing up. I'll almost certainly feel better once I shift, but I have to get to that point first.

After a soak in the tub, I feel slightly more alive. I immerse myself completely in the water, and emerge with a splash.

"Time to head down to the prison wing," the droid sings. "Shall I show you the route myself?"

"Please do."

I dry myself gingerly, and shift into my lion form. My lion can handle this hangover from hell. He's way stronger and more resilient than his royal alter ego.

One day. One day of working like a little person. That's all this is. I can handle one tedious day with shitty company.

Tomorrow, I'll be back to my carefree royal life. And the good times will roll once more.

And no more bets with Reago. That's for damn sure. Well, not unless I'm sure I'll win. He can kiss my ass if he thinks I'm going along with any more of his stupid ideas.

Shaking my mane and growling softly to psych myself up, I pad after the droid, all the way down to the prison wing.

"Just get us the hell out of here," I yelp.

"You got it," my ship's computer Neela replies.

Neela switches on the supplementary emergency harness, and it flips itself over me. I'm now pinned in my seat, unable to reach the controls. It makes sense to leave the getaway strategy to Neela, because she's AI and serene, and I have a puny human brain that's freaking the fuck out right now.

"Engaging warp speed."

Oh boy. This is going to get messy. My ship probably hasn't hit warp speed since before my grandparents were born. I can't be sure it's going to hold out. But we have no choice. We have to try.

The floor vibrates beneath my feet. Vibration quickly turns to shuddering, then shaking. I hold on to my secondary harness with trembling fingers.

We're flying so fast, the coordinates screen has gone blank.

"Heading into open space," Neela says, calm as a summer cloud.

I'm lost without my pilot screens on. The whole ship undulates and rattles, like a giant toddler picked it up and is waving it around.

"Are we losing the Imperial Order ship?" I yell.

"No."

There's a certainty to Neela's voice that really scares me. I mean, there's no tone at all in it, because she's not real. Obviously I'm projecting tone onto her words, because I'm the one who's terrified of being caught with stolen goods, and because I can't stand the thought that I'm in this much trouble all by myself. But either way, my heart rate is through the roof again. And Neela can't calm me this time. All the meditation in the world isn't going to fix my current problem.

"So they're still following us?" I ask, gritting my teeth.

Please say no. Please say they just went another way.

"They appear to be following our course exactly, at a distance of approximately one kilometer."

"Oh God." I shut my eyes and try to think clearly. "Have they sent any communications?

Maybe they just want to check our flight permit or something?"

"No communications. I will try to initiate a link." Neela goes silent for a moment, and then speaks again. "I am unable to connect with their computer. Their mainframe will not accept the connection. It is therefore likely that they wish to meet with you in person."

I want to hide my face in my hands and yell, but what's the point? It's hopeless. We're never going to outrun them, even if we do travel at warp speed. Imperial Order ships can fly way past that velocity anyway. We're like a kitten trying to outrun a cheetah.

We're doomed. And by *we*, I mean *I*. However much I adore Neela's company, there's only one lifeform on this ship.

The screen flickers back on, and I get a good perspective on open space. The blackness stretching out in front of me looks like sweet liberty.

"How's the rear view looking?"

Neela swaps the camera aspect so I can see behind us.

I whimper as the entire screen is filled with the Imperial Order ship. "They're hot on our tail, Neela."

"Correct."

"We can't escape, can we?"

"The odds of our managing to escape now are one in seven hundred trillion."

"That good, huh?"

"Maximum period of warp drive engine use now reached. Warp drive engines deactivated."

The turbulence tossing the ship around seems to subside. It feels like we're gliding on water now. Neela pulls the camera focus back so we can see more of our pursuers.

"The Imperial Order ship has locked on," she says.

My spine feels like icicles just slid down it. "Locked on?"

"They are pulling us into their gravity field."

"Shit. Neela, we have to do something." I struggle against my emergency harness. "Get this thing off me." Neela obeys.

My fingers work fast, opening up the communications panel and activating my fingerprint identification. I speak into the microphone. "Greetings, Imperial Order vehicle. What is the nature of your inquiry?" My words are instantly converted to their language, and I hit Send.

I stare at the screen, willing the reply to be *"Sorry ma'am, just a case of mistaken identity. You're free to go."*

Instead, there is nothing. Silence. The lack of a reply feels worse than a hostile one. And then the gravity pull begins.

The first tug backwards throws me forward, and I scream. "Get the harness back on me, Neela."

There is a second, and a third, and a fourth tug. It feels like my ship is being sucked into a black hole. Or a vortex. Not that I know what either of those really feels like.

"Preparing to dock on Imperial Order ship," Neela says in a slightly bored voice, like she's waiting for her nail polish to dry so she can eat her M&Ms. "The system will shut down in ninety seconds."

"What?" I gasp for words, unable to formulate language for a moment. Then reality comes back to me. "Shutdown? Neela, what the *fuck*? What are you doing?"

"The Imperial Order ship is operating a vacuum procedure. The system must shutdown to preserve essential circuitry. Imperial Order over-ride in operation. System shutdown in sixty seconds."

"Neela, how can you be shutting down? I'm not authorizing a shutdown."

"System shutdown in forty-five seconds."

"Do not shut down," I order her.

"System shutdown in thirty seconds."

"I'm the commander on this ship," I bellow, but apparently this means zero to my artificial pal. When she announces the twenty-second warning,

I kick the flight desk. It doesn't help, and it leaves a black streak on the trim.

"System shutdown in five seconds."

"Neela, don't go," I holler.

It's pointless. With one last flash of the flight desk panels, the ship is plunged into darkness.

There's no way out of this. I've been absorbed into an Imperial Order ship. I may never be seen again.

I think quickly. Is there any place I can stash the chip? Probably not. If they find it somewhere on this vehicle, I'll be punished just the same as if they find it on me. I decide to just leave it in the unscannable compartment in my boot, in case I get lucky and they want me for some other business.

The ship stops moving, and I realize it must have docked. Nothing's happening.

I call out into the blackness. "Okay mother-fuckers. Are you coming to get me, or what?"

The door release clicks, and a white light appears around the edges of it. The door descends slowly. I squint to see who's standing there, but the light is so bright, I can hardly make it out.

When I finally get my eyes to focus, they almost pop out of my damn head.

There's a lion at the bottom of the stairway.

A lion.

A lion.

"*There are lions in space?*" I screech, even

though there's nobody to hear me except the freaking lion.

It takes my brain a good few seconds to realize that this is an Imperial Order shifter. He just happens to be shaped like a lion right now. Of course.

He's an impressive beast. And he's an honest-to-god *lion*.

"Holy shit," I whisper, as the lion leaps toward me.

4 JALTON

I prowl around the female, who cowers in her seat. She pulls her legs up and hugs them close to her, like that's going to stop me attacking her.

Humans are idiots. If I'd planned to attack her, I could have destroyed her entire ship from a distance. But I guess she doesn't know that.

She also doesn't know I'm just moonlighting in this job for today, and really couldn't care less about any of it. I only plan to do a quick checkover here, and then move on to the next prisoner in line. If she gives me any trouble, I'll roar at her, or something. That ought to keep her in line.

The female is very pretty in a disheveled sort of way. She has a sulky pout, hourglass curves, and wild tangled auburn hair. I like the look of her already, even though I know she's a criminal. She's easy on the eye.

But I don't stare for too long. No point pursuing my interest. According to Kaljo's helpful Imperial Order Prisons 101 explanation last night, she's likely to be either locked up or executed before the day is out.

As I turn to survey the ship, my lion nose detects a metallic, elemental scent I can't identify. That's strange. Technology from another world? The scent is not from Earth, although this female is definitely human. And it isn't from any of the main planets in the galaxies surrounding us either.

A quick visual sweep reveals nothing but ancient human electronics and computer circuits. Yet the alien technology scent persists.

Intriguing. I need to know more.

I sniff the air, and the human freezes. Tracking the scent around her seat makes her squeak in terror.

The scent is more concentrated around the floor. I glance over it to see if there are any compartments or storage facilities leading down from the floor panels, but there are so many patched together that the job would be impossible. Easily dismantled, when the wrecking crew strips down the ship later.

Irritatingly, I the mysterious metallic odor is also masked by an artificial fragrance wafting around the ship's interior. It carries the scent profile of Earth-based floral plants.

Humans and their dumb perfumes.

A quick tour of the whole flight deck takes seconds, because the ship is so narrow. The exterior casing is laughably fragile. I find it hard to believe this vehicle can even fly. It would be shredded in an asteroid storm.

"What do you want?" the human says. Then a thought seems to light up her beautiful face. "Oh, wait. You're an Imperial Order shifter. You probably don't speak English. Let me feed that through the translator." She opens up a tab on her ancient screen and begins to shout into it. "What? Do? You? Want?"

I'm tired of this already, so I stand still and will myself to shift back into my two-legged form. I need to talk to her, and she'll be less freaked out by my words if I'm on two legs and not four.

Immediately, I stand before her, my skin now stripped of golden fur. To her, I must look like a human man. Only much taller, and broader. Human men are tiny and feeble. Their muscles are flimsy as an eyelash. Mine are sturdy and strong, as they should be.

"Don't bother with the translator," I say. "Were you harmed by the ship transportation process? Do you need any medical assistance?"

She jumps, as though my words gave her an electric shock. "You can speak English?"

"I speak all languages in this galaxy and the two hundred surrounding it. Don't you?"

She's staring. She can't stop staring.

"Nnnn...no," she says, at last. "I use the translator app. I didn't... I don't..." She breaks off, still gawping at me with that wide-eyed expression. She can't take her eyes off my body. How curious.

"Why are you regarding me with such intensity of purpose, human female?"

She clears her throat. Her eyes do not move from my central zone. "Dude. You're... ." She clears her throat again. "Oh, come on. You're butt naked. What the heck?"

Apparently humans know nothing of shifting. Such a strange, bewitching creature, with her luscious curves and empty mind.

"I just shifted," I say, incredulously. "And clothes don't shift with me. It isn't rocket science."

It was going to be a long morning.

After I catalog this scrapper and give her a code, I'll still have another eleven captured ships waiting in the docking bay. Can I get away with leaving some of them for the real prisoner warden team? I don't want to break a bet, but this shit is getting time-consuming already. Usually I'd still be in bed, or sitting down to a leisurely five-course breakfast.

"Well, okay," she says, pursing those pink lips again. "Yeah, perfectly normal to be standing in front of a woman you've never met with all your manly goods on display. Because you're a *space lion*. Of course. Yeah, what could be weird about that? I mean, why would a guy bother getting dressed? Especially when he's a lion. In space."

We have a feisty one here, I think to myself as I reach for her touchscreen. "This won't take long."

"What won't?"

"I need to catalog you."

"*Catalog* me? What am I now, a *specimen*?" Her voice has gotten higher and squeakier. "What is it you want from me anyway?"

I lay a hand over her touchscreen and it springs to life. All vehicles in the tri-galaxy have an Imperial Order override function. It's a legal requirement. The service droid told me this morning. With a few swipes, I find the ship's serial number and the pilot's flight credentials.

"Name: Commander Corby Frayne. Place of birth: Minneapolis, United States of America, Earth. Age: 26. Confirm these details please."

"That's me. Who's asking?"

I pat a few more commands into the screen interface. It's ancient technology, but I've seen worse. "I'm Prince Jalton."

"You're a prince?"

"That's what I said."

"Right." She nods, then looks back sharply. "Wait, they send princes to interrogate lowly freelance couriers? Who does the important stuff? Janitors?"

"I lost a bet with my brother." I frown, irritated that I'm being drawn into personal conversation. "Okay, Commander Frayne. You'll need to come with me."

"Sure. Do you plan to slip into something a little less comfortable first?"

"Stop talking. I said follow me."

I shift back into my lion form, because that's what I'm supposed to be today. It's what the prison wing expects. Corby Frayne looks dubious, but she rises from her seat and follows me, at a slight distance.

The door to her ship remained open after I entered. I pad through it and down the stairway, looking back to check she's following right behind me. She is.

"Where are we going exactly, Your Royal Highness?"

I don't respond. I can of course speak in animal form, but she probably doesn't know that. Having shifted means I can ignore her human babble for the time being, without any objections. She doesn't ask again. Our short journey is blissfully peaceful.

The long corridors are pretty empty. We pass a few of my colleagues, some in clothed humanoid forms, and some in the forms of their animals. Commander Frayne mutters words of surprise under her breath whenever someone is in their animal form. Her childlike wonder is remarkable. Presumably she has had little experience of consorting with the Imperial Order.

I cannot even imagine living a traveler's life like hers. My entire world is inside the Imperial Order. For a few seconds, I allow my mind to drift. What would it be like to live outside the Order, like a Wildcat, never sure of the next job or the next meal? It sounds at once thrilling and horrifying.

We reach a bank of interrogation suites, and I take her inside one of them. I leave her there and step out again, closing the door behind me.

"Wait, where are you..."

The door locks, with a soft bleep.

A junior enforcer appears in the corridor, and almost jumps out of his skin when he sees me. My class is very rarely found on this workers' deck. His pale cheeks turn pink and he bows deeply.

"Oh. Wow. Hey, Prince Jalton. I was just... Did you...?"

"Get me some clothes. Also, I need refreshments suitable for a human. I have a prisoner to process, and then I'll be heading back up top. You'll need to arrange for somebody else to deal with the other prisoners. Change of plan."

He's still startled, so I add "Now," which sends him scuttling off to obey my order. He doesn't ask why I'm processing prisoners in the first place. He's used to us princes and our stupid japes. He's also paid to obey us.

Fortunately, he returns almost immediately with some clothes, and a tray. I shift back to my man form and then throw on the outfit, which is only two pieces of custom-fit tailoring and easy to slip on. Both pieces fasten automatically, so I take the tray from him and let the fabric do its thing.

"Pleasure to serve you, Your Highness," the underling calls out. I don't bother responding.

When I return to the room, the human female is not sitting in the chair provided. Instead, she paces the floor, skipping up and down and humming a tune. I stand in the doorway watching her for a moment. Eventually she realizes she is being observed, and stops.

"They need to put a bell on that door." She chews her lip, looking furtive.

What does she have to hide?

"I'll make a note of your suggestion," I say, setting the tray on the table.

"Hey, is that drink for me?" She lifts up the glass, looking confused. "It's pink. What is it? Cherryade?"

"It's water."

"Why is it pink?"

"Humans drink colored water."

"No we don't. We drink clear water." She sniffs it suspiciously. "Or soda. Soda can be colored. Is that what you were thinking of? Soda?"

I've tuned out her questions already, so I sit opposite her, with my touchscreen panel in front of me. "Okay, let's get started. I have a lot of ships to process today, so I need to wrap this up as quickly as possible." I don't mention that I'm going to bale out after this job.

"Tastes like water. Weird that it's pink though."

"You've been hauled in for..." I check the screen. "A series of outstanding traffic violations."

Seriously? I'm dealing with this sort of crap? Inwardly, I curse the losing bet that sent me here.

"A *series*? No, man. No way. I have *one* unresolved violation. One. Left the ship in a no-fly zone on Drancolia. That's it, I swear."

"It says here that you have a total of forty-one outstanding violations. Plus one historic offence committed when you were under the age of majority, for which you are still on probation."

She nearly spits out her pink water. "Forty-one violations?"

"No mention of the Drancolia rap either. That will bring it to forty-two."

"No, no, no. This can't be right. Are you sure you don't have me confused with somebody else?"

"It's not possible for Imperial Order technology to mix up two pilots. Your DNA is sequenced when you are assessed for your flight license."

"Look, I don't know how it's happened, but it's happened. I have *not* committed forty plus traffic violations. That's nuts. Check again."

"It's unnecessary."

"Please?" She looks desperate. Her long eyelashes flutter as she blinks back tears.

I don't know why, but I decide to indulge her. "All right." Restarting the search takes fractions of a second. The whole thing runs again, but comes back with an identical table of data. "It's all the same results as before. Forty-one violations, not including the Drancolia ticket or your juvenile record."

"Let me see that."

She almost leapfrogs the desk and leans over the screen, frowning at the list of offenses. Her long hair dangles onto my lap. It smells of Earth flowers and herbs. I breathe in her fragrance, momentarily off-guard.

It occurs to me that I've never been with a fully human female. It's been a while since I was with any female, in fact. Too long. Our father insists that I marry Lady Simla, so most women don't dare to accept my advances. They'd literally be killed. I understand, but it doesn't mean I don't wish things were different.

The women of Drancolia are beautiful to look at, but they never smell as good as this Earth girl does right now. Corby Frayne's fragrance reminds me of exotic fruit, ripening in the twin suns of a Ganidroke morning.

My lion stirs inside me. It wants her. It's a demanding animal. But it's not getting its way this time.

"Uh, Your Highness? Why are your eyes closed?"

I snap them open at once. "It is irrelevant. Listen, are you sure there's no way you forgot you had all these outstanding charges?"

"*Forgot*? Yeah, sure." She rolls her eyes at me. "Once you get over forty violations on your record, it probably sticks in your mind."

I scroll down the list again. Some of them do seem unusual. This isn't my real job, so I can't be sure, but the wording on some of them seems odd. Hasty, perhaps.

I read out one of the charges. "*Two counts of exceeding the speed limit on Ninklobia.* Sound familiar?"

She leaps up, almost bursting with the urge to speak. "Ha! I knew it! These charges are all bull-shit. There is no speed limit on Ninklobia." She sits down again, folding her arms triumphantly. "Something's up here, Prince Jalton. I'm being set up. And that's your proof."

I look at her, and then back at my screen. Then I perform a quick search on the device for the Ninklobian speed limits. And... she's right. I look up at her and back at the list. It doesn't make any sense.

I tip my head forward, massaging the back of my neck. It still aches from the all-night casino session. A complicated case is the last thing I need. I was only supposed to jump in, do some boring work to repay my gambling debt to my brother, then return to the royal wing. Now I'm expected to fix a screw-up too?

"Look, the computer doesn't make mistakes," I say, at last.

"Okay, sure. Then like I said, somebody's setting me up. Either way, I'm innocent."

"That's ridiculous."

"It is, isn't it? But now you know, you'd better let me go."

"Nice try." I read the entries again. "What I don't understand is how you weren't hauled in long ago. Forty-one violations is a lot."

"Exactly. That proves it's bogus. Your Imperial Order guys are thorough. They don't wait for someone to commit their forty-second crime before they jump on them."

The human makes a good point. How had she slipped through the net? Could there be any truth in her claim that she's being set up?

She leans down to tug her bootlace tighter, and her hair falls in a curtain over her face again. The enticing floral scent wafts across the air toward me.

"Commander Frayne, I have no idea what's happening here," I say, in my most official voice. "But it's not something I have any interest in pursuing. I need to process you, and then I'm out of here."

To hell with it. This is definitely my only job down on the interrogation deck. Enough's enough. One super-demanding prisoner was enough for me. My brother could forget the damn bet. I'd repay him some other way.

"You don't care that an injustice is being done?" She opens her eyes wide, and locks onto mine. "You don't care about what's *right*?"

"Save the theatrics, Commander. You Wildcats have no morals at all. Let's not debate that, by the way," I add, because she opens her mouth to speak again. "I have one job to do. Then be back in the royal quarters, and I'll leave you in peace."

"Leave me in peace where?"

"In the cells, awaiting justice."

She yelps in anguish, and a weird pang flits across the muscles of my stomach. Before I can analyze it, there's a knock at the door.

"Yes?"

"Prince Jalton, the floor manager has an update for you." It's the junior enforcer from earlier. His face is scarlet, and his hands tremble. "Please read this."

He passes me a note, written on paper sealed

with a wax-stamped crest. The only time communications are done that way is when it's top secret. Only paper messages are untraceable, and unhackable.

I unfold the paper and read it. It's written in the Zsiatin language, an obscure method of hieroglyphics taught only to Imperial Order natives.

The note is short and simple.

"Kill this prisoner," it says.

And underneath that, it says "Do it off-world." It's signed by the head of the Imperial Order discipline wing.

I look at the enforcer, who smiles meekly. He has no clue what's in the note. He wouldn't be shooting me shy grins if he did.

I read the note one more time. Holy shit.

This communication was meant for a real inspector, someone way below my class. Someone who apparently has the task of killing prisoners without trial when ordered to. Is that how we conduct our justice system? Apparently it is.

The sender of the note had no idea a prince would receive it.

Nausea returns in a rush. I press the back of one hand to my mouth as I contemplate my next move.

There is no need for me to get my hands dirty with this kill. In fact, it would be most inappropriate for me to do it. The best thing to do would be to pass the job back to the real criminal processing team. That way, I could get my royal ass back topside, and stop meddling in other people's jobs. That's what I've been wanting to do since I got here, after all.

I look at the prisoner. She stares beseechingly at me still, with those wide hazel eyes.

My lion moves inside me. My blood stirs with longing for her soft human flesh. My lion roars, and it will not be quiet.

I already know what I have to do.

A deal is a deal. I lost the bet, so responsibility for this prisoner falls on me.

I fold the note up again and tuck it inside my hip pocket.

"I'll take care of it," I say.

The junior enforcer nods, and I close the door.

5 CORBY

Prince Jalton closes the door on the messenger guy, and remains standing. "We're moving. Get up, Commander Frayne."

"Where are we going?"

It's like I never said a word. He opens the door again and says "Follow me," in his deep grouchy voice.

The good news is that he's staying in his guy form this time. No more lion. The lion was gorgeous, but also kind of terrifying. I'd never gotten so close to an apex predator before.

The bad news is that all his pretty man parts are covered up with clothes now though. Boo. It's a little bit of a tragedy. The tailoring works too, but he looked jawdroppingly incredible in absolutely nada. And I'm aware I probably shouldn't be looking at an Imperial Order prince like he's a hot studmuffin, but sue me. I'm in trouble anyway.

There are no more options, so I follow him like he wants me to, down long winding corridors lined with blank windows. I'm pretty tall, but his legs are way longer than mine. The man is huge, and *fast*. Before long, I find myself jogging just to keep up with his casual stride.

"Where are we going, Your Highness?" I say. Kissing his ass with the *"Your Highness"* part is irritating, but I can't afford to piss anyone else off today. I get the feeling my Teflon coating is wearing thin.

Again, he doesn't turn around. He just keeps moving.

Finally, we reach a set of doors. Prince Jalton places his face up close to the screen, and it must operate a security scan or something, because the doors open almost instantly. I stay close behind him, in case they slam shut again. He's authorized, and I'm obviously not. Although he must be allowed to take prisoners wherever he likes. He's one of the princes, after all.

Prisoners. I shiver to think of myself as one of those.

How am I ever going to get out of this predicament? I have no money even to pay the damn Drancolia fine. I definitely can't cover any of the other made-up charges. This serious. If I can sweet talk my way out of any of this, it'll be a miracle.

And if the rumors are true that Imperial Order prisoners are usually executed if found guilty, no matter how minor their crime?

Shit shit *shit*. I'm so screwed.

We're in a dark spacious room now. I can just about make out where the walls are, because they're accented with tiny bulbs in rows like perfectly arranged fairy lights. But I can't see what kind of a place it is.

Before I can ask Prince Jalton about it, the main lights in the room switch on.

My jaw falls open when I look around. It's a vast rocket garage. Rows of what look like eyewateringly expensive ships take up the center of the space. Way in the distance, I see one wall is stacked with weaponry, while another is filled from floor to ceiling with touchscreen devices of one kind or another. Scanners, sequencers, whatever. I have no idea. Imperial Order technology is way ahead of my puny hardware.

Finally, the royal roarer decides to talk to me. "We're going on a little journey," he says, like it's a daytrip to the beach.

"Excuse me?"

He leads me to a particularly sleek looking ship, and opens the door with another face scan.

"A journey?" I say, panic starting to rise. "I'm not stepping inside that thing. If I'm going anywhere, it's going to be in my own damn ship."

The entry staircase descends with a soft whoosh. When it has extended fully, he turns to me. "Please step inside. This won't take long."

A deep sense of foreboding grips me. Folding my arms in front of me, I stand with my heavy boots apart and shake my head. "Nope. I'm going nowhere."

He looks at me, as though seeing me for the first time. Frowning, he shakes his head slightly, as though his ears may be blocked. "What?"

"I said I'm not going in there with you. Something bad might happen, and..." I falter. "I can't leave my ship."

"You already left your ship."

"Only for a conversation. Which turned out to be a lot more of a ballache than I expected. And anyway, it's not like I had a lot of choice. You barged in, like a... a lion. But this?" I wave my arms around manically. "This is a whole other vehicle." I take a step back. "Why would I need to get on this particular ship? What do you have in there?"

"I have no idea what's in it. I just need to take you elsewhere, and this looks like a good vehicle to take for a spin." He shrugs, with the natural confidence of a guy born into unimaginable privilege. "I can take whichever one I want. Are you going to stand there arguing, or are you going to follow my instructions?"

"Do you plan to take me somewhere in this ship? Because let me tell you, that is not okay."

He looks me up and down, his eyes running languidly from my face down to my feet and back again. I feel a flush of awkwardness at his attention. He's stupidly good looking, and I can't stop my cheeks burning. Damn this royal jerk.

"Look, you're going to have to trust me," he says, but his face is totally unreadable.

He doesn't meet my eye now, and instead just holds the door open for me. I don't know the guy at all, but I'm still getting a vibe that suggests he's not being upfront with me. Who knows what the real deal is?

"What if I resist?"

He shrugs. "Well, I could always shoot you right here and now. That's probably what they do to prisoners resisting arrest." A ghost of a smile plays around the corners of his mouth.

"Arrest? You're not an enforcer."

"No, but I'm sure princes can arrest people too. And shoot them."

"Oh, really? You're sure?"

"Of course. Who's going to stop me?" He flashes me a full-beam smile for the first time, and it throws me off-center for a moment. He's even more handsome when he's not frowning. "Look, just get on the ship, Commander Frayne. I don't have time for this. If you value your career, I suggest you do as I say."

"And if I don't?"

He holds eye contact steadily. "If you don't, you have forty-one chances to tell the authorities why you disobeyed me."

I pause for a second, thinking about all my options.

Then I realize I'm out of options.

With a little squeak of frustration, I begin to climb the stairway.

Prince Jalton hurries me on to a sleek looking ship and hits the door close panel. The ship is way more fancy than mine. In fact, it's on a whole other level of fancy. Mine looks like an antique go-kart in comparison.

This one has what looks like a marble and steel interior, trimmed with precious alien stones that glimmer slightly in the soft lighting. I don't know if this is standard decor for Imperial Order ships, but somebody put some real effort into making this comfortable. Prince Jalton is a rich boy, obviously, so he probably doesn't even notice. But to a kid from a blue-collar Earth neighborhood, this shit is *fly*.

"All right," he says, settling himself on a luxurious chair at the flight desk. "Here's what we're going to do."

He gestures to a chair further away from the controls, but no less comfortable-looking. I sit.

"I'm told that I need to take you off-world," he continues. "So that's what I'm going to do."

"Why?" I sweep my hands through my hair, partly because I'm nervous and partly to pull it back off my face. "Who told you that? Why would you need to take me off-world?" I begin to panic about out-of-galaxy torture centers and execution ranges. "That sounds like you have me down for something serious. I have traffic violations, not murder charges."

"You have forty-two violations. That's pretty serious."

"They're all minor crimes! Not big-ass felonies. Nothing to justify taking me to one of those... far away places."

"You're admitting to the forty-two violations now?"

"No!" I sigh exasperatedly. "We're going around in circles. I did not do *any* of that. Except for the Drancolia parking thing, like I said. And the, uh, the juvenile record. Just those two. Nothing else. I just meant... oh, never mind."

A screen emerges from the flight desk and he touches it lightly a few times with the fingertips of both hands, like he's playing a piano. Immediately, the engine starts.

"Sit back," he tells me.

The safety belts engage, much more smoothly than on my ship. I feel slightly guilty for being so impressed with another ship's algorithms. Poor Neela does her best. I'll be extra nice to her once I get back on board my own ship and restart the mainframe.

Please let me get back to my own ship, I silently beg the universe.

I'm not sure how it works but we somehow manage to launch into space, despite our ship having been inside a sealed room *on another ship*. Imperial Order skills, man. These guys are smooth operators.

After a few minutes of flying, I decide it's a good time to ask more questions.

"Prince Jalton, you have to tell me why you were told to take me off-world." I smile sweetly. "Uh, please."

He doesn't reply for a moment. Then he says "No, I don't."

"Dude! I mean, Your Highness. This is unfair."

"It's just a statement of fact. You said I have to tell you. I don't have to do anything. I'm a prince."

He says all this in a calm matter-of-fact way, like he's telling me the time.

The chip is still hidden safely in my boot, but I don't know for how much longer. If I don't tell anyone about it, what if I'm killed?

What if the chip is lost forever?

What if the people depending on me never find out what happened to me? And never get the information I was trusted to bring to them?

I can't escape this situation. I can't smuggle the chip out of here, any more than I can fight an Imperial Order shifter. There's only one course of action I can think of.

What if I confided in the Prince?

Ordinarily, speaking truth to power is my last choice. But I'm down to my last choice right now. Either he's going to kill me, and it won't make any difference, or he's not going to kill me. And if he keeps me alive, there's maybe a one percent possibility that he'll help me.

Telling him about the chip is definitely not something I want to do, but it's all I have. It's my one backup option. I'll think about it.

His eyes are still on the navigation screen. I could be doing anything back here. I cast my eyes around for any sign of something I could use as a weapon. Just in case things get nasty. Man, I hope things don't get nasty.

Plus, would I really want to damage that

perfect face of his? Now that really would be a crime.

Silently, I order my ovaries to quit doing the tango just because I'm up close with a handsome man. They're not helping.

We're in open space before he swivels his chair back around to face me.

"I'm going to level with you, Commander Frayne."

"Please do," I say, fighting to keep the nervous tremor out of my voice.

"I know there's something you're not telling me." He scrutinizes me closely, like he did before, and a flush of warmth creeps over my skin. "Something big."

"Why would you think that?"

"Because you were picked up with a frankly ludicrous number of outstanding misdemeanors on your record, which just doesn't look right."

"Okay."

"Because you smell nervous."

Guess animal shifters have the same super senses as regular animals. I didn't realize I actually *smelled* nervous. Sounds kind of gross, really. I shift in my seat, embarrassed in case he thinks I stink. Although why the hell should I care what he thinks? I shouldn't. But I do.

"Right."

"And because you're so jumpy, you look like you're hiding something."

"Anything else?" I say, trying to regain a little of my old attitude. It's not really working, but it's better than nothing.

"Like what?"

"Any other reason you *just know* I'm not telling you something? Or should we put it down to good ol' male intuition?"

"Okay, yes. There's another reason," he says, pulling out a slip of paper from his inside pocket. He narrows his eyes at me and pauses just long enough for my heart to start pounding. "It says here that I must kill you. I'm guessing there has to be a good reason for that."

She freezes, like a prey animal just before the hunter lands its fatal blow. Then she recovers herself.

"Hell no. Safety harness *off*." It springs back automatically, and she seems taken aback that the command worked. She runs to the door and pounds it with her fists. "This is not happening."

"You realize we're in space? You really want to open the door?"

She turns, her eyes blazing. "Are you kidding me? You brought me off-world to *kill* me? You bastard."

She abandons the door now, launching at me with her fists instead. Pure rage flashes in her eyes. I grab her wrists and hold them up safely over her head. It's not remotely difficult. Humans are pretty weak, and I include trained fighters in that assess-

ment. This female is stronger than average, I esti-
mate, but her physical force is still nothing
compared to mine.

On the other hand, she's kicking me hard with
her heavy boots, and it won't be long before she
lands a blow that makes my eyes water.

"Whoa there, Wildcat. I said the note told me
to kill you. I didn't say I was going to obey it."

She stops struggling. "What?"

"The note orders today's inspector to take you
off-world and kill you. And what I want to know
is: why?"

"*Why?*"

"Why does the Imperial Order want
you dead?"

"I have no freaking idea at all."

"None?"

"None. I'm innocent. I keep telling you."

Her arms go limp in my grasp now. I let her
hands drop, and she doesn't try to hit me again.

I look at her closely, noting the way the ship's
artificial light hits the soft angles of her face. "You
see, there is something strange about your situation,
Corby Frayne. It really doesn't add up. I don't see
how a lowly Wildcat racked up over forty traffic
violations without getting caught. And even if
they're real crimes, they're minor ones. I don't
understand why any of them makes you important
enough to kill."

"I'm not important enough to kill. I'm nobody."

"But that's clearly not true either. So tell me, Commander Frayne." I settle myself back onto the pilot seat. The angry woman stands before me. It brings us a little closer in height. "What exactly does the Imperial Order know about you that I don't?"

She kicks at an imaginary mark on the floor, with a sulky expression. "You tell me. You're the prince with the *execution order*."

"Whoever wrote this order didn't know a prince would be dealing with it. They thought it would be a regular inspector. And they would never give background information to one of those."

"So why don't you just call your daddy? I'm sure he'll authorize a full database search."

"My father takes no part in such petty matters."

"Executing criminals is petty?"

"Of course."

She rolls her eyes, which somehow makes her even more likeable. She's not phased by my royal status. If anything, she seems to think *less* of me for it. That's a new experience.

"You're nuts if you think I'd tell you anything." She pouts again, and the insolent curve of her lips gives me inappropriate thoughts. "You'll just kill me the second I finish talking. Or hand me over to someone else to do the dirty work."

"No, I won't."

"*Riiight.*" She draws out the word to enhance its sarcasm potential.

I grip her by the shoulders, and she bites her lower lip, looking up at me rebelliously. I feel the gesture in my pants.

"I said I'm not going to kill you, Corby Frayne. You're going to have to trust me on that."

She snorts in derision.

I mean what I say. I'm not going to comply with the order. Not a chance. That kind of mindless brutality gives the Imperial Order a bad name. Once Corby Frayne has told me her big secret, I'll just take her back to the cells, and explain to the officer in charge that I used the royal prerogative to pardon her. That should clear everything up.

And maybe then I'll...

I silence my own imagination. It is unseemly to be thinking of making advances to a person of such low birth. It would be an abuse of power. My lion must give way to royal protocol, whether it wants to or not.

It really does *not* want to.

We fly in silence for a while. Corby Frayne twists her hair around her fingers. It's not a coquettish move, as far as I can see. She looks genuinely anguished. I want to do something about that, but I can't. She's hiding something, and we both know it. And I am certain she is never going to give up her information without a fight.

And then out of nowhere, she starts talking.

"I stole something. Something really important."

I keep my eyes on the monitor screen. If I don't look directly at her, perhaps she'll be bold enough to keep telling the story. "Okay."

"Half the galaxy would kill to get their hands on what I have."

"I don't doubt that." Of course, she actually meant the stolen item she's carrying, rather than her bombshell physique. This probably isn't the time for lame jokes. My bad.

"Anyway," I say, when the pause gets too long. "Continue."

"Somebody almost died to get it out of a total hellhole. An even more repressive regime on another world. I've been tasked with taking it to Quintagon. Someone is waiting for it."

"I see." The hairs on the back of my neck prickle. "What is the thing you stole?"

She takes a deep breath. I notice I'm holding my own breath too. This has turned into quite the suspense thriller.

"It's a chip."

I exhale. "A chip? That's it?"

"You're disappointed?"

"I'd guessed it was priceless Keeluko art, or rare gemstones at the very least."

"This is not just any chip. This one contains comprehensive information about Imperial Order corruption."

I blink. Imperial Order *what?*

"And it's big," she continues. "Huge. The documents go all the way back to the last century. The murders, the illegal trade wars, the manipulation, the funding of atrocities. It contains enough information to bring down the entire Parliament. This stuff is red hot. I'm pretty sure that is why you were told to kill me." She rubs her temples with both forefingers. "I don't know how they know I have it, but they must. An enforcer tried to pick me up just before your mothership did. I guess I already knew I was in trouble."

She stops and watches me. I'm aware that my reactions are under scrutiny, so I try to adopt a neutral face.

It's difficult. I don't recognize anything of the things she's telling me.

"Imperial Order corruption?" I manage to say at last.

She snorts. "Right, because you don't know anything about that stuff."

I frown, shaking my head slowly. "Seriously? You think the Imperial Order regime is corrupt? How can that be so? We've ruled this cluster of galaxies for two hundred years. We couldn't have done that if we weren't straight down the line."

"Is this another joke?"

I look blankly at her. "Why would it be a joke?"

"The evidence is pretty clear, *Your Highness*." She says this last part in a contemptuous tone. "I'm shocked that you're even acting innocent about it. You think it's all unicorns and rainbows in the Imperial Order? You think we all adore you, and welcome your boots stamping on our faces? Then you really don't have a clue."

Her "we're all equals here" irreverence simultaneously baffles me and makes me hard. I concentrate on suppressing the latter thought.

"Okay, fine. Where is this legendary chip now?"

She smiles. "Well, now. That's the question, isn't it?"

"It is, yes. Answer it, please."

"I don't have to do or say anything. You can't make me."

"Technically, I can. I'm a prince. And you're a citizen. And you're on my ship."

She scowls and makes an angry noise. I sit back and watch her. She's astonishingly beautiful, if you can catch a glimpse of her face under the tangled mop of hair.

"It's not your ship. You just borrowed it."

"All property in this sector ultimately belongs to the Royals."

She makes a loud "Ha!" noise, then frowns. "If I tell you where it is, will you keep the information to yourself?"

"No. How could I?"

"Then you can forget it."

I rub my eyes, unable to stifle a yawn. The late night is starting to catch up with me again. "Look, I can fly you around the stars all day if that's what it takes. But what's the point? We both know there's only one way out of this. Just tell me the damn location, and I'll take you back to the Imperial Order ship."

"But I don't want to go back to the Imperial Order ship. I want *my* ship, and I want to get the hell out of here."

"Your ship is *on* our ship."

"Then get it *off* your ship, and give it back to me." She puts on a deep voice, mocking my royal accent. "Technically, you can. You're a prince."

Before I can respond, there's an incoming call from the command center. "Yes?" I say to the air, in my own language.

"Jalton?"

"Uncle Mirodag?"

This is freaky. What's my uncle doing, calling this ship? How would he know I was on it? I didn't send that information to anyone on the main vessel.

In fact, I'm acting completely against orders just being out here with the prisoner. So obviously I hid my movements. Even if there's a tracker in this ship, how does my uncle know I'm on it?

Maybe it's a coincidence. Maybe Uncle Mirodag makes a lot of calls to small spaceships in the area, and it's just pure luck that it happens to be the one I'm flying. It's not likely, but nothing about this day makes any sense.

"Family?" Corby Frayne mouths at me, suddenly silent. I nod.

Could Uncle Mirodag have started operating the command center? That sounds implausible too. He is far too senior for such trivia. On the other hand, a prince shouldn't be doing any of this either, so I guess we're even.

Either way, it's somewhat disorienting to hear him right now.

He, on the other hand, doesn't sound at all surprised to hear my voice. So he must have known I was here. *How?*

"What are you doing there, Jalton?" he asks, in a calm tone.

"I lost a bet. Long story."

"And did..." There's a long pause. Now his voice drops, low and urgent. "Are you dealing with the Frayne matter... in its entirety?"

"Yes. Of course."

"Did you..." Another long pause. "Did you dispatch the prisoner?"

"Dispatch?"

I assume he means *kill*. And since when did Uncle Mirodag take any interest in crime and punishment matters?

"Yes or no, Jalton?" he asks, his voice oddly urgent.

I lock eyes with my prisoner. She wears that anxious expression again. My heart squeezes against my ribs.

"Everything is taken care of," I say, shaking my head at her to let her know she mustn't speak. "What was that all about anyway?"

He huffs and puffs for a second. "I may as well tell you, since you're now involved. Although I don't understand why you didn't walk away the moment you realized you were dealing with something beyond your understanding. You must have known the communication you received wasn't intended for you. Others are employed to deal with law enforcement matters, Jalton. It's most inappropriate for you to involve yourself."

"Like I say, I lost a bet with Reago." I roll my eyes for Corby's benefit, so she knows I want to close the call down, and she smiles weakly. "What do you mean 'beyond my understanding'?"

Uncle Mirodag still uses his low conspiratorial voice. "The prisoner smuggled a dangerous packet of information across enemy lines. The contents are incendiary." His voice drops even lower. "I don't want to alarm you, but... in the wrong hands, they could bring down the entire Imperial Order empire."

I watch my passenger, as she stretches out her arms and legs, and bends down to touch her toes. "How interesting."

"A little knowledge is a dangerous thing, Jalton. It's all falsehoods and propaganda, of course. But it's well-constructed propaganda. The girl was a terrorist and had to be stopped. I'm sorry you had to deal with it, Jalton. But we are where we are. I daresay it will make a man of you."

"Sure," I say, feeling a little nauseated again all of a sudden. Killing Corby Frayne seems even more impossible than it did already.

My stomach rumbles, and the thought of last night's Aloyishan rum makes me want to throw up. If only I'd eaten a full breakfast to soak it up.

With effort, I concentrate on my uncle's words.

"Did you perform the kill in your animal form?" he asks.

"What? Oh, uh, yeah." Yeah, why not. I'll let them think my lion tore her to pieces. That's about as logical as anything else right now.

"Good. Make sure there is no trace of human blood on your fur. Return to the Imperial Order vessel by moonset, please."

"Got it."

He hangs up at this point, so I do the same.

Corby Frayne leans forward, flicks her hair back, and stands up straight again. I shake my head disapprovingly. "Terrorist? Really?"

"Who, me?"

"Who else? My uncle Mirodag assures me you're a danger to us all."

"Mirodag? Prince Mirodag? Ha." She laughs mirthlessly. "He's just saying that because I have some really bad stuff on *him*. Him in particular." She folds her arms. "Your uncle's an asshole. Sorry, but it's true."

I shrug. It sounds credible. "Let's get back to the point. Where's the chip?"

She pulls her wild mop of hair off her shoulders and twists it into a crazy-looking knot on top of her head. "Why did you protect me?"

I open my mouth to respond, but I'm not sure I even know the answer myself.

Why did I lie to my uncle for her? I don't approve of pointless killings, but saving her has put me in the firing line. Lying to the Imperial Order is as bad as betrayal. They won't kill me for it, but they could make my life a misery.

It would have been a lot easier just to walk away from the whole thing, like Uncle Mirodag said.

If I didn't want to kill her myself - and I sure

didn't want to do that - then why didn't I go back to my own life and let the system deal with her? Or just go straight to the top and issue a royal pardon? Why am I involved like this?

"I'm not sure," I say at last, truthfully. "There was just no way in hell I was going to kill you for a bunch of traffic violations. And there was no way I could allow you to be killed for a crime that doesn't even make sense to me. That's all."

There's a kind of battle-worn yearning in her eyes that makes me long to reach out to her. But I don't. She'd probably try to shoot me and take over the ship, if I did.

"So where are you taking me now?" she says, chewing her lip again. She directs her eyes away from me.

"Tell me where the chip is, and I'll tell you where I'm taking you."

I punch in some coordinates with my back to her, so she can't see where we're headed. She makes another of her irritated exclamation noises, and then sighs melodramatically.

"Okay. All *right*. I'll tell you." She indicates herself, with her thumb. "The chip is here."

"Where?"

"Somewhere on me. That's enough information."

"You'll have to be more specific."

"Well, I'm not going to be."

"Do I have to check over every inch of you to find it?"

The awkward pause that follows crackles with tension. My cock twitches as I imagine conducting a fingertip search.

"Not necessary," she murmurs. There's a long silence, and neither of us moves. Then she makes an exasperated noise. "Oh, to hell with it. Okay. It's in here."

She sits on the co-pilot seat and rests a boot on the other knee. Touching the side of the thick sole, she locates whatever invisible thing she's looking for.

Then she taps it three times. A little tray opens, holding a chip.

"It's here. The chip that could burn your whole world to the ground." She takes out the chip and holds it up. "It's here."

He looks genuinely astonished. "How did you get that past the scanners?"

I palm the chip and pat my boot. "Undetectable, unscannable. The coating of this little compartment is made of a super advanced impregnable material. It was developed on Freeoth in secret. The inventor gave the blueprint to the resistance."

"The Resistance?"

"The people who oppose your family's rule." Prince Jalton looks at me blankly. "You do understand that a resistance organization exists, right?"

Prince Jalton nods vaguely, but it looks like his mind is blown. How could he not know about the Resistance?

"Why are you telling me this?" he asks.

"Because I know you risked a lot to save my

life. And you didn't have to do that. And honestly, I'm still not sure why you did do it. But I owe you something, and knowledge is all I have to give you." I sigh. "No, okay, that's crap. I told you because you'll just rip me limb from limb to find it anyway, or kill me and use my bones as chopsticks, or whatever you Imperial Order maniacs do. At least this way, I have a chance of not ending up as lion food."

His eyes glaze over and he frowns slightly, like he's thinking all this through. "So why didn't the guy on Freeoth tell everyone about his unscannable material invention, and license it? He'd make a fortune."

"I guess because *she* felt the Resistance was a more important cause than money, and *she* sacrificed potential riches to help. I expect that kind of decision-making seems totally incomprehensible to a royal like you." I can't resist one last jab. "Just like the idea that a shit-hot inventor could be female."

"Ah. The inventor's female. I get it." He has the decency to smile at his own error. "Okay. Sorry."

"So are you going to kill me now?"

He pats his rock-hard abs. "I can't concentrate on life-and-death questions while my stomach's growling at me. Are you hungry, Corby Frayne?"

I'm super suspicious, but also starving. "Kind of."

"Great. I'll check the food stores." He lays his hands on the command panel and stands up. "You know, this is not how I imagined today would go when I awoke."

"No? What did you have planned for your royal day, Your Highness?" I don't even bother to hide the snark in my voice. He smiles wryly, and he looks even more handsome than he did already.

"This was supposed to be my punishment. I lost a bet, and a card game. And now here we are. I'm in space with a terrorist thief, battling the hangover from hell, with my corrupt uncle on my ass. Or at least that's what you tell me he is." He surveys the walls, and throws up his hands in disbelief. "Where the hell did they put the food storage compartments on this vehicle?

"Well, you're not stuck with me." I lift my chin defiantly. "You can call into the Imperial Order ship and get my little vehicle sent to meet me on whatever the nearest planet is. And then I'll be out of your hair."

"I can't do that."

My fingers beat out a nervous rhythm on my thighs. "You know you can."

"You know I can't. You'll be executed instantly if the enforcers find you. The head honcho issued an order. The warrant will be valid intergalactically."

I swallow, feeling suddenly lost. I fight the urge to ask the big guy to hold me.

"Then what *are* you going to do?" I half-whisper.

"That's a good question."

"I know. Answer it."

"I'm going to eat. And so are you."

"*Please.* What are you going to do with me?"

He stops patting the walls and stands tall in front of me, with his hands behind his back. "The obvious thing to do would be to complete the kill. Or take you to some gun-for-hire who'll do the job without tainting my royal hands. My uncle would say those are the only possible choices."

I feel my knees wobble. They're going to buckle underneath me if I'm not careful.

We look at each other for a while. I can't read him at all. His face is open, and his eyes seem honest and decent, but... he's still a part of the *Imperial Order*, for crying out loud. How much can a person ever really know about these pedigree wackjobs?

Finally, I speak. "So what's the plan, Your Highness?"

"I'm going to take you someplace where you can go into hiding. You, and your controversial chip."

I'm floored. "Why... why would you do that?"

"Because it's the right thing to do."

"I..." I look away, then back at him. Emotion

overwhelms me, like a tidal wave. "I don't even know you. How do I know I can trust you?"

Stepping forward, he takes my face in his hands. I blink away a stray tear.

"You're right," he says. "You don't know me, Commander Frayne. You don't know anything about me. Apparently you don't know much about the royal family at all. And I know nothing of you." He looks at my lips, while still holding my face. I'm breathing too fast. Then he meets my eye again. "I'm everything you despise, and... well, you shouldn't even be a blip on my radar. But here we are."

I close my eyes, just letting his firm touch strengthen me. I shouldn't let an Imperial Order bastard touch me, not even a sexy one.

But it's been so long since anyone held me. With no family and no friends left alive, life is a constant struggle.

This guy may be full of shit, but right now, right in this moment, he's all I have.

"How?" I whisper. My voice is scratchy. "How am I going to make it if I'm in hiding? How do I survive if I can't go to work?"

He looks me deep in the eyes, and strokes a lock of hair off my forehead. For just a second, it feels like he might kiss me. But of course he doesn't. I feel stupid for thinking it.

Does he mean what he says? Is an Imperial

Order royal family member really capable of taking me out of this nightmare? How will I know if he's sincere, or just stringing me along so he can get me killed later instead?

"You're just going to have to trust me," he says again.

"How can I?" I whisper.

"What choice do you have?"

He's right. It's either put my fate in the hands of this mysterious prince, or give myself up.

"Then fine. Take me away from all this, Your Highness," I sigh, closing my eyes again. "I'm all yours."

For a while, we fly in silence. Prince Jalton makes himself busy dealing with the flight controls. I stare at the navigation screens, trying to keep my stress levels in check.

I can believe he was ordered to kill me. The whole organization is psychopathic. Besides, they won't let me get away with treason. If they know I have the chip, execution is the least they're going to do with me.

What I *can't* believe is that Prince freaking Jalton is going to defy the order and save me. I mean, what's his motivation? Why would he help me? Surely he'll make his own life too complicated by doing that? It'd be so much simpler for him to pass me on to someone lower down the scale, who can finish me off, just the way they want.

I shudder to think of it. Whatever his crazy fucked up reason for helping me stay alive, I'm grateful.

It's scary that he knows where the chip is now though. I had no choice, but I wish I hadn't had to tell him. Sure, he's being nice now. But can he really keep the information to himself once all this is over?

He's Imperial Order. The ties run deep. Whatever he says now, sooner or later he's bound to want to know who's betraying his family. And he'll need to keep a lid on the scandal that'll happen if any of it becomes public knowledge. Royals don't just help Wildcats out of the goodness of their hearts. Their hearts are a goodness-free zone, for a start.

"We still need to find the food stores," he says, breaking my train of thought. His beautiful sculpted face is solemn. "All this talk is making me even hungrier."

"Oh. Yeah, right." Guess the subject is officially changed. I was running out of energy to deal with it anyway.

I look around the space. What kind of food is stored in here? Maybe it'll be old school freeze dried rations. Maybe it'll be top quality Imperial Order-worthy fine cuisine. Only one way to find out. I don't realize how ravenous I am until my stomach lets out an anguished rumble.

"You too, huh?" he says, with a smile. "Now where did the ship's engineers intend hide it all?"

There's a shallow recess in one wall panel, pretty low down. Not expecting much, I pat it tentatively. To my surprise, a square door opens.

"Well, whaddya know?" Prince Jalton looks delighted. "Nice job, Commander."

I curtsy, like a goof. We kneel down in front of the open door and I pull out a tray filled with silver boxes, marked with unfamiliar symbols. Below that shelf is what looks like a thick glass cube. I don't recognize the technology, so I just look at Prince Jalton.

"That's for heating the food," he says. "Wait a second, I'll take a look." He comes over and peers at it. "I never used one of these myself on a flight before. We always have..." He breaks off.

"You always have servants to do that stuff, you mean?"

He shrugs. "Well, yeah. Busted. But look, it can't be too difficult. Some of these vehicles are only meant for a couple of people to fly in. Those guys must be doing their own catering." He says something in a language I don't recognize and the front of the glass cube opens. "There you go." He studies the silver boxes and selects two. Then he slides them into the cube. A few more strange words, and the cube closes itself.

"Wow," I say. But before I can even ask him about the symbols or the language, the cube opens again. The scent of delicious food wafts out. My mouth waters, and my stomach practically flips over with eagerness.

"Dinner is served," he says, taking out the boxes.

"What is it?" I ask, even though it doesn't matter. It smells so damn incredible, I'm going to eat it even if it's something gross. Like snake eyes, or moldy bugs. *Anything*.

He tells me the names of the dishes in that same weird language, so I'm no wiser.

"Okay," I say. "Whatever it is, I'm down for that."

Prince Jalton ushers me to what looks like a kind of breakfast bar, with pullout seats I never noticed before. We sit down next to one another. The silver food boxes flip open to reveal compartments full of what looks like the best Italian-Asian fusion food ever, and I groan as the aroma hits my nose. It's the best food I've ever smelled in my life. There's a fork-like utensil tucked into the edge, and I copy Prince Jalton when he slides his out.

"You don't have one of these on your ship?" Prince Jalton says, gesturing to the panel now hiding the glass cube thing again.

"Nope. I don't even have a microwave."

He frowns, as though he doesn't know that word. "What do you eat?"

"I eat cold packaged crap. Or freeze-dried powder meals I, uh, *borrow* from clients' ships. Or I stop on a friendly planet and try to sweet talk someone into buying me dinner. Or I beg for leftovers at the Wildcat canteen."

He laughs. "What an interesting life you have, Commander Frayne."

"That's one way of putting it."

It's sort of cute when he calls me by my full title. And speaking of cute... I'm trying hard not to look at him that way, but damn. *Damn.* Even shoveling alien cuisine into his mouth, the man looks like a male runway model. It's unreal.

Bad idea to let myself think like that, since he's a prince and I'm probably lower down the pecking order than his shoeshine boy, but... yeah. He is hot as hell. My body just keeps on responding to his presence, whether I like it or not.

We eat in companionable silence. Occasionally I break it with an "ooh", or an "oh boy, this is good", but mostly I'm just trying not to think about my predicament. The food is a great distraction.

It's been a while since I ate so well. The taste lives up to the incredible aroma. I can't believe convenience meals intended to be eaten in the sky could be so delicious.

"Hey, why were you so hungry?" I ask, when I have just a couple of forkfuls left. "Didn't you eat a twelve-course breakfast this morning, back at the palace? Served by nubile handmaidens, on golden plates?" He looks up at me and I wink. "Just a normal morning at your place, right?"

"Not quite," he says, raising a single eyebrow. "Let's just say I had to be forced awake, and I skipped breakfast."

I don't ask why he didn't want to get out of bed. Probably had a woman in there. For some reason, this makes me feel prickly and irritable.

He clears away our plates and tips everything into a recycle chute, which appears as if by magic out of the tabletop.

"I want to know more about you," he says, all of a sudden. The intensity of his amber gaze hypnotizes me. I'm floating in the clear pools of his eyes, for just a moment.

I snap out of it. "What, are we friends now? Come on." He looks mildly offended, so I hurriedly add "There's nothing to tell. Tell me all about you."

"Oh, I've had a very boring privileged existence."

"Privileged is not boring to me. That's exotic."

"Exotic?" He laughs, a real belly laugh that makes me grin too. I can't help myself.

"Of course it is. I grew up in a poor Earth family. We didn't live like you do. I'd love to know more about it." I feel my cheeks warming as he gazes at me, so I look down at the marbled floor panels.

"Do you see your family much?"

I swallow. "They're not around any more."

"Oh, I'm sorry."

"It's okay. You didn't kill them." I bite my lip to hold back my feelings. "Your family's space army did that."

His smile drops and he looks mortified. "I am so sorry. So very sorry." He takes my hand and holds it. He's warm, and his big hand almost swallows mine up.

I feel kind of awkward about how much I'm enjoying holding hands with him, so I don't meet his eye. I don't want to think about my family either.

"Tell me about you," I repeat.

"Okay." He does something to the flight desk control panel with his other hand, which I assume means engaging it in autopilot. "Where do I even begin?" Turning back around, he folds his free arm and leans against the edge of the desk. He doesn't drop my hand.

I watch the pattern of star clusters on the monitor screen. It's beautiful. "Begin anywhere. Go."

"How far back?"

"Wherever you're comfortable." I catch sight of

a small chunk of space debris floating past. Luckily it was a long way away from our ship.

It's so relaxing, sitting here with him, holding hands. I'm starting to lose that pent-up fear feeling. Things seem kind of... nice.

He opens his mouth to begin his tale.

And then I see it. There, on the screen.

Danger.

Before I even register in my conscious mind what it is, I let out a scream. Prince Jalton jumps fully to his feet, on red alert.

"What's up, Corby?"

I register dimly that he called me by just my first name, but that doesn't matter right now. Words seem to have left me. I'm still capable of pointing though. So I point to the monitoring screen behind him.

He spins around, and sees what I see.

There's a ship on the monitor. And it's not an Imperial Order ship this time. It's much worse than that.

It's Kreapers. The deadliest space pirates in this multigalactic zone. Their red-alloy ships are legendary in the galaxy. It's rare to see them these days, but they still operate. The entire galaxy lives in fear of an encounter.

The only people who can speak of them are those who ran for their lives and got away. If they capture you, it's all over.

Nobody has ever been caught by Kreapers and lived to tell the tale. *Nobody.*

"Is that what I think it is?" he says, his voice suddenly urgent.

"Yes," I manage to squeak. "Kreapers."

"You know what that means?"

"They see us. They're locked on to us." I see the gun barrels raise up out of the Reaper ship flank, just as he does.

"Presumably we can't get away before they shoot."

"No we can't. We're screwed."

He pauses for a second, and then he sits down in the pilot seat.

"No," he snarls. "No way. Not happening." The lion is suddenly visible behind his face. He growls, a low, deep rumble that vibrates in my spine. "What is *wrong* with today?

"But—" I begin. He doesn't let me finish.

"Fuck them. No. Not on my watch." He jabs at the controls and calls out "Prepare weapons" to the ship's computer. He indicates the seat next to him. "Sit down, Commander."

I obey immediately, my stomach fizzing with horror and dread. The Kreapers seem to have snuck up on us out of nowhere. They're so close. If we can get away in time, it'll be a miracle. I already know it's not my lucky day.

Prince Jalton prepares to fight them, and I sit next to him, paralysed with dread.

"We're taking these bastards down," he says. "Here goes."

8 JALTON

It is fortunate that we had finished eating before the Kreaper crew decided to mess with us. Filling my belly seems to have brought me back to life again. My hangover is almost gone. My lion roars with righteous rage.

The Kreapers will not win this time. How dare they mess with us? They will regret their foolish error.

The ship we are using is small, and it's possible they mistake its small size for vulnerability. But it is a technically advanced piece of engineering. It is not the kind of ramshackle vehicle Corby Frayne uses to roam the stars. That one would be helpless if attacked.

Why the hothead wants to return to a vehicle like that, I have no idea. I will look into providing her with a new one. Perhaps she can keep this ship, if it does not become too damaged by the fight we are about to have.

Perhaps the Kreapers have every confidence that they can take over our ship and wreak whatever terrible havoc they wish. That is the nature of thugs, and thieves. But they picked the wrong ship today.

It's not going to happen. I will not allow it.

I will not put Corby Frayne in harm's way for a single moment.

I pat the edge of the control panel a few times. "List contents of ship's armoury," I say aloud.

A hologram appears, with a rotating array of weapons. Good. The ship is pretty heavily armed. I'm not convinced even the largest guns could take out a Kreaper vessel instantly, but they could certainly do plenty of damage. That might be enough to convince the Kreapers to pick on somebody else. If not, I'll try something else. I will not rest until they are defeated.

"What are we going to do?" Corby says, sounding anguished. She gets up again suddenly, as though she might bolt somewhere. But there is nowhere for her to go.

"You really are going to have to let me handle this. Please sit down. Perhaps you would be more comfortable out of range of the viewing monitors."

I nod my head toward a crew seat in back, but

she returns to the co-commander chair next to me, with a peevish look.

"Well, all right then," I mutter. She may as well sit where I can keep an eye on her.

"What shall we do, *Your Highness*?" There's that sarcastic tone again.

"We?" I say, glancing at her for a second as I prepare the heaviest duty laser rays. "First of all, please call me Jalton from now on. Royal formalities are pointless in this situation. And second of all, there is no 'we'. You're not participating in this battle. You've never even been inside a ship like this before, let alone handled the guns."

She makes a snorting noise which, if I'm not very much mistaken, sounds like she's laughing at me.

"Oh please, Prince Hoity-Toity. *You've* never been in a battle before, in *any* kind of ship. Right? I'm going to go out on a ledge here and say I don't think you've ever been in combat your whole life."

"Not true." I think about all the fights I had with my brothers growing up. Some of those were brutal.

"Fistfights with siblings don't count."

"Look, you're not operating the weapons on this ship, Corby. They're serious firepower."

"Dude, who do you think you're talking to? I live and breathe weaponry. Let me take a look at this." She scoots over to the control panel and peers at it.

Her leg presses against mine, and she doesn't move it. I know I should edge away to give us both more space, but the fragrance of her wild hair and her peachy skin is captivating. Breathing in her unique human scent, I memorize its high notes, its base notes, and the slightly vanilla undertone. She still smells fearful, but there is strength in her. She has a heart of steel.

The warmth of her thigh stokes a fire in my body.

"Are you listening to me, Your Highness?"

Her irritated tone jolts me out of my sensory reverie. "I said call me Jalton. And of course I'm listening. Look, we don't have time for a discussion. The Kreapers are gaining on us."

"And once they lock on close to a target, they're near impossible to shake off. That's why they're every pilot's worst nightmare."

"It's great that you're thinking so positively about this, Commander Frayne." I take the manual control stick in my right hand and hover my left over the armory panel. "That's just the kind of blue-sky thinking we need." Two can play at sarcasm.

"Whatever. Listen, Jalton. Do you have any acrobatic flight experience? Like, did you pull the kind of stupid stunts most teenagers do when they first get your pilot's license?"

"God, yes." I think back to my younger days, when Reago and I were learning to fly. We got up to some unbelievably stupid shit. Our mother was permanently in a state of high stress. "I know my way around a three-sixty loop."

"Great. So here's our plan. You fly like a bat out of hell, and I'll shoot 'em up."

"That's our plan?"

"You have a better one?"

I think about it for a moment. If she's right about her weapons experience, maybe she is the best choice of armory operator. I can handle this sleek ship. Okay, I was banned from combat duties because of my royal blood, but I aced my space fleet military service.

I nod. "What the hell. Let's do this."

The armory control panel is wireless, so I move the entire thing over so it's in front of her.

"Engage pilot and co-pilot combat harnesses," I say out loud to the voice command sensors. The straps cross over us and hold us steady in our seats. We're going to need those, if I really let rip with the stunt moves.

I engage the manual boosters. "Hold on tight, Corby," I say, with supreme understatement.

"On it." Her face is stern. Her delicate jaw is set firmly to *don't fuck with me*.

I prepare myself mentally for a sharp steer, and

then act on it. The ship lurches violently to the side.

"Doing okay so far?" I ask, not turning away from the navigation screen.

"I'm good," she says. "How do I engage these—no wait, I got it."

As our ship darts around in space, Corby Frayne blasts ammunition at our pursuers. The Kreapers are about to get a lot more than they bargained for.

The first laser jet streams miss the Kreapers, but that has more to do with my deliberately jerky steering than with Corby's aim.

The second blast she sends out hits the ship square in the left gun flank.

"Fuck, yes," she shouts, already sending a second stream from the other side of our vehicle. This time, she fries the entire front of the Kreaper ship's bodywork.

"You've done this before," I say, spinning the ship around and flying it upside down at 180 degrees from our previous flight path.

"Guilty as charged," she says. Then she realizes what she's said. "Wait, I'm only guilty of that though. Not the other bullshit forty-two charges. Move!"

I snap the reverse on and shoot us backwards at high speed, just as a Kreaper bomb jet explodes in front of us. We narrowly missed that by an unimaginably tiny fraction of time.

"That was close," I say.

"Sure was, Prince Obvious."

I can't help but smile at her terrible attitude. It's probably the first time anyone has talked to me like this. And it's outrageously hot. Nothing sexier than a bit of spirit, when everyone has kissed your ass your entire life.

The Kreapers seem to be on the back foot, but I know that can only be temporary. I pull the steering around so we're now hovering parallel to their ship, with our nose pointing away from the nearest planet. With any luck, they'll think we're about to dart forward, to make a break for open space.

"Do we have any serious laser power on this thing?" she asks.

I glance at the control panel, then back at my own controls. The Kreapers are hovering too. They probably think they can catch us if they just wait to see which way we're going.

"This is a fourth-generation ship, so it must have the Laser Atomizer function. It's hard to get right though."

Her lips pucker in delight. "Laser Atomizer. Ooh, I like the sound of that. Where do I find that one?"

I take another quick look at the Kreaper position. It does seem to be constant. They're waiting for us to make our move. Grabbing the control panel, I slide it back over to me and check the screen.

"There. See the square marked with that symbol? Like a circle with two lines through it? That's all the Atomizer jets. You'll have to scroll through and see which ones you want. Then you need to hit the timer just so, or it vaporizes."

"Is there any way this thing can display the names of each gun in English? I don't speak symbol."

"Sorry, no. We all have multilingual brain software. Translation functionality is not something that's relevant to us."

She makes an exaggerated groaning noise, and I smile again.

"You know, I'm not sure I've ever met anyone like you, Commander Frayne," I say, as I guide the ship slowly around.

"Ditto."

She pats the control panel, and a blue plume of laser fire shoots out of our ship. On the monitor screen, I can see it doesn't connect with the Kreaper ship.

"Shit." She recalibrates the gun. "Align the two guns together, *then* load up the targeting sensor. Got it. Sorry Jalton, what did you say?"

"Nothing." I address the voice activated control

again. "Locate nearest wormhole. Prepare ultra drop boosters."

"Ultra drop? That sounds like we're going to whizz right out of the sky or something."

"Is your harness on, Corby?"

"Yeah, you know it went—"

"Hang on." I touch the red triangle on the screen and it starts.

Our ship shoots down a wormhole leading toward the nearest planet, which the tracker tells me is Skoogmel. Never been there. Hope the restaurants are good.

"Oh... my... god..." squeals my co-pilot. She can't say much else, because the gravity force pulling us into the seat makes it impossible to speak.

I concentrate on keeping my head still. The ship is moving so fast down the wormhole, the monitor has stopped showing pictures and has instead become just a black rectangle of nothingness.

This ship has a good range of emergency moves, and the Kreapers' ship is clearly a lot older. If luck is on our side, we'll be out of range of their sensory equipment before they can get a second lock on.

The hurtling seems to go on for ever. We feel as heavy as a planet ourselves, being sucked downward at warp speed, like a rock being thrown off the Flagatrovian mountain range.

At last, our descent begins to slow. The ship vibrates a little, and I take that to mean we're approaching the atmosphere of Skoogmel. If we can get through this part without burning up, we're good.

Our velocity is now back within the usual flight range, so I can move my limbs again. The first thing I do is take Corby Frayne's hand and hold on tight.

"Asshole," she hisses.

"Sorry. Better than being torn limb from limb by the Kreapers though."

Corby Frayne simply makes an "ugh" sound in her throat, and I give her hand another squeeze.

We blast through Skoogmel's atmosphere with no trouble at all. It seems a pretty thin layer. According to the flight desk meters, we barely lose any of our external fireproofing.

"What now?" Corby says, releasing my hand. "Where are we? Also, next time can you tell me what you're doing before you shoot us like a bullet across space?"

"Things happened pretty quickly. I didn't really have the opportunity to describe the emergency escape function in much detail." I pull up the Skoogmel guide on my screen. Then I look back at her. "Wait a minute, *next* time? You want to fly with me again?"

"Well, you said you were hiding me, remember?

So you'll need to take me someplace else after." Then her eyes widen. "Oh my god. You were planning to leave me here on this planet?" She looks a little alarmed. "Where are we? What kind of place is it?"

I don't want to admit I don't have a fully-formed plan at all yet, so I opt for a mysterious shrug. "Let's find out."

The Skoogmel guide shows us shots of the planet taken from various latitudes. It seems to be made up mostly of dusty arid plains, with hardly anything growing. It's a backwater.

There won't be anywhere to hide Corby here. She'd be easy pickings for anyone who traced her. We need a more urban environment, where she can blend in with all the other intergalactic citizens.

Just as I'm about to prepare the landing protocol, there's a bleep from the ship's computer. "Fuel low. Please refuel."

"Okay, so we need to refuel," I say aloud, without thinking. Then I turn to Corby. "Excuse me for being Prince Obvious again."

"Let's hope they have rocket fuel on this planet. What's this place called?"

"Skoogmel," I say. "And we're going to touch-down right about..." I pause as the reverse engines power on, slowing our drop to the planet's surface. "Now."

The ship glides to the planet's surface smoothly. I'm feeling pretty pleased with the way things went.

Whatever we're about to find, it can't be as bad as the things we're running from.

Nobody has that much bad luck in one day. Do they?

9 CORBY

"I'm not so sure about this place," I say, as I edge down the stairway.

My legs are still jello from the ridiculous high speed escape we just did. It just shows me what an old gal my ship is. I'm not used to any fancy moves, or locating hidden wormholes. Yes, it was my idea to fly like crazy people to get away, but I didn't know quite how drastically Prince Jalton would interpret that idea. Glad he did, though. Otherwise we'd be Kreaper snacks right about now.

"Are you hungry?" he says, stretching his long arms, one right behind my head.

"What? No. We just ate." I look at him quizzically. "Wait, you're hungry again already?"

"I have a healthy appetite," he says, with a lazy grin.

For some reason, his words send a little prickle

across my flesh. Damn. I can't afford to keep noticing how hot this royal mystery dude is. He's the enemy. He might be helping me now, but who knows how things will turn out? Not me. I'm never going to trust someone from the Imperial Order. I'd be stupid if I did.

We look around for a moment, getting our bearings. Jalton taps a device on his wrist, then nods. "Okay, there's a refueling plant about one hundred vaylons from here."

"Vaylons?"

"How do you humans measure distance? I forget."

"Miles, usually. Maybe kilometers. Depends where on Earth you're from."

Jalton frowns, and shakes his head. "We'll stick with vaylons. And it's this way."

He starts to walk, and I don't move. When he turns to see why, I point at the ship. "We're not taking the thing that needs fuel to the place that sells fuel?"

He looks nonplussed. "Of course not. Someone will come and fill it up where it is."

"Oh dear. Buddy, you have a lot to learn about the non-royal world. I don't know how they do things here on Skoogmel, but I'm not convinced it works like that outside your royal bubble." I beckon to him. "Come on. Let's fly the ship to the fuel place. That way, if we need to do our own refueling, we're right on the spot."

He looks skeptical, but he follows me back on board and starts the engines. It only takes a few minutes to fly to the refueling station.

The station is situated right on the edge of a dusty desert, and it looks like the kind of place you'd drive five hundred miles to avoid. Still, we don't have enough juice left to be choosy. So we have to just make the best of it.

In the middle of the plot is a shack made of something that looks a lot like wood, painted dark green. There doesn't seem to be anyone inside. We hang around outside for a moment, looking in all directions.

"Hello?" I say tentatively into thin air.

Jalton calls out some weird shit which may or may not be the language of this planet.

"Are you talking Skoogmel-ish?" I ask, slightly impressed, even though I don't want to admit that.

He says a bunch of other stuff in what sounds like more than one language, then he swaps back to English for my benefit. "No. I don't know which language, or languages, they speak here. Until someone arrives, I'm just trying out a few possibilities."

"You're pretty clever, for a super privileged jerk," I say.

He laughs. "You're pretty charming, for a tangle-haired criminal."

"Yeah yeah." I can't help smiling, even though I try to look fierce. This dude's personality is starting to grow on me. So he's not just a pretty face. Maybe royals don't have as much of a stick up their ass as I thought they did.

Just as I'm starting to think we won't get any kind of service around here, we hear shuffling noise. It seems to be coming from behind the shack.

A creature emerges, and I've never seen anything like it. I yelp by accident, then concentrate on staying still and quiet. The creature addresses us, and Jalton talks back to it in whatever the hell language it is.

I just watch quietly, because I'm apparently I'm just a clueless human around here. Not that I mind. The guy - I'm calling it a guy, but who knows? - well, he has a kind of orange octopus-shaped head. Little wavy tentacle things move constantly around his face. His nose looks like a shorter version of a baby elephant's trunk. He's big and round, with four orange-bronze arms coming out from the front of his shirt, and he shuffles on big flat feet. I'm torn between staring at him, and hiding my eyes.

The conversation with Jalton seems to be going well. He takes him into the shack, and beckons for me to follow. Jalton catches my eye and nods. Hesitantly, I step inside, and immediately wish I hadn't. The smell of rotting vegetables is thick in the air. I clap my hand over my mouth and stagger out.

Octopus Head barks something at me, and Jalton says something which seems to smooth it over. There's no way I could survive another second in that stench. How can Jalton stand it? Imperial Order men really are superhuman.

They must have agreed terms, because after a few minutes, they both come out of the shack again and bow to one another. Octopus Head claps, and some smaller versions of him run out. I step back instinctively, but Jalton comes over and puts his arm around me.

"He's selling us some fuel?" I say, trying not to breathe through my nose.

"He sure is. Even though he says it's really hard to get a full tank on this planet, for any price. Lucky I managed to change his mind."

"Wow. Aren't you the smooth talker?"

"Apparently so."

Jalton's arm feels good around me. Without stopping to think about it, I match his gesture by putting my arm around his waist. He looks down at me, with a smile.

"Good idea. The arm. Yes. I told him you were my new bride, so it's probably best we do this kind of stuff."

"You said what?" I stare at him. "Why would you say that?"

"You heard me. He said there was no fuel. He said he wouldn't even take gold bars in return for the supplies he had. So I told him we were newly-weds and had broken down here, and needed fuel to get to my family home so I could present you to my father. Then he suddenly remembered he had a stash of fuel for emergencies."

"Whoa. I have to give you points for creativity. And also for excellent lying. That's kind of discon-certing."

Octopus Head is shouting at his mini-me troops. Two are filling the fuel tank and the rest seem to be doing random polishing of the ship's exterior.

I nudge Jalton in the ribs. "So you didn't tell him you're Imperial Order royalty?"

He hushes me with an urgent "Sshhh. If they find that out, they'll cut off a body part and send it to my father as a ransom note. The Imperial Order isn't popular on the outer planets."

"Or anywhere," I muttered. There was a lot to think about when you were royal. "All right then. You're just Joe Anybody. I get it."

"That's right. And you're the beautiful Mrs. Anybody. Let's stick to that until we get out of here."

"Beautiful, huh?" I punch him playfully, until I

see he's gazing thoughtfully at my face, and not smiling. Then I just blush furiously and turn away, kicking pebbles with my boot until my face stops burning.

It takes something like fifteen minutes for the fuel tank to be filled. We stroll around the edge of the desert with our arms around each other, playing the happy couple. It's strange, but it doesn't actually feel that wrong. Jalton's waist fits nicely in the curve of my arm, and his hand feels just kind of right on my shoulder.

It's been too long since I was with a guy, and that's why I'm enjoying it so much. That's all this is. I keep telling myself that.

Jalton pays Octopus Head with some gemstones from his pocket. I didn't know he carried gems. Is that a royal thing, or an Imperial Order thing? Is that what they use as money? Who knows.

"So are we leaving now, or did you want to do a little sightseeing?" I ask.

We exchange bows with Octopus Head, and the tentacled one sings us what I guess is a song of congratulation. I smile and bow again, and hope that's the right thing to do.

"Well, I was hoping to sample the local cuisine," Jalton says, "but it doesn't look like they'll have the kind of restaurant I'd want to take you to. So maybe we should hop to the next planet and see if we have more choice there. Maybe there's a cock-tail bar."

"You want to take me out for cocktails?"

He smiles to himself and turns away, like he doesn't want to tell me what he's thinking.

"I'm starting to think you can stand my compa-ny," I tease.

"Listen, why don't we continue this conversa-tion in the air? There's a cluster of planets around 60 grangs from here. If we hurry, we can make it there for dinner."

I'm not even going to attempt to ask what grangs are, so I hold my hands up like "Whatever you say", and follow him. He steps aside for me to take the stairway first.

Before I reach the top, Jalton shouts "Run" at me. I almost fall off the stairway.

"What is it?" I hiss.

But he can't answer. Suddenly, we're surrounded by a bunch of creatures, who are stamping and making whooping noises. It's the mini Octopus Heads who just refueled the ship. Big Octopus Head is nowhere to be seen.

"Can you get inside the ship?" Jalton hollers. He doesn't turn to look at me. He's keeping his eyes on the mini Octopus Heads.

"The door's closed," I say in a small voice.

Whatever these creatures want from us, it isn't good. Their faces are all screwed up and wrinkly.

They look mad. Jalton isn't armed, so this standoff is alarming to say the least.

I still have my crappy gun in its holster, so that's going to have to do the job.

Jalton says something to them in their language, and one of them replies.

"What did he say?" I ask.

"You don't want to know."

"Yes I do." Anxiety pings through my veins.

"He told me 'Your uncle is very displeased with you'." Jalton's mouth is set in a firm line. Anger radiates from him.

"Oh fuck."

"That's my thought too."

"Your uncle is sending hit squads after us?"

"Looks that way."

I gasp. "Oh my God. The Kreapers...?"

"Yeah. It was pretty weird that they appeared out of nowhere in that stretch of empty space. I'm starting to think perhaps my uncle has friends in some dark places."

"What are we going to do?" I move my hand very slowly toward my gun. If I don't make any sudden moves, maybe I'll be able to reach it before the mini Octopus Heads notice.

"Give me a moment," Jalton says. Then he speaks to them again in their language.

I keep slowly reaching for my gun.

The main mini Octopus Head answers Jalton. His fists clench.

"No," he snarls.

Before he can lunge at the hostile aliens, I jump from the middle of the stairway to the bottom. I overreach and accidentally crash into Jalton, and he staggers but recovers quickly.

Fortunately, the sudden move confuses the mini Octopus Heads, and I take that split second opportunity to push my gun into Jalton's hand. I'd shoot them myself, but he's taller and there are too many of them for me to shoot them from this angle. He'll get a better reach than I would. And I kind of owe him for letting me shoot last time.

Let's hope he really can handle it. If he turns out just to be a pampered rich boy who can't shoot straight, I'm wrestling that gun back and shooting them all myself.

He doesn't say a word, but takes the gun. I use the element of surprise and punch the main mini Octopus Head in the face. He falls over backward, burbling furiously.

More aliens charge us, and I kick a couple of them out of the way. They're not all armed, but the ones who are seem to have a nice shiny ray gun each. Way nicer than mine, by a factor of about ten billion. Oh boy. Let's hope they don't know how to use them.

By now, Jalton has full control of my beat-up-but-still-functional gun. His height and strength work in his favor, as he manages to take out the first row of five or six creatures in seconds.

I pick a small one up and try to use it as a shield. It's floppy now, though, so it slithers out of my grasp.

"Just keep shooting," I shout, as I elbow a mini Octopus Head in the face.

He does exactly that. Right up until the moment when my piece of shit gun jams, and stops firing.

The mini Octopus Heads sing songs of triumph in close harmonies, and form a circle around us.

"Fuck," we yell in unison.

"Now what?" Corby says to me.

"I was about to ask the same question of you."

Stuffing the now useless lump of steel into my belt, I make a mental note to carry a gun wherever I go from now on. A working gun. As it turns out, these things are useful. That's something you don't notice when you have servants doing everything for you, from morning to night.

Then again, it's only today that one of my family members decided to kill me and my travel companion. That doesn't happen to a guy every day.

Uncle Mirodag is not going to get away with this.

And he's not going to kill Corby Frayne either. Nobody is. My lion will rip everyone in the galaxy apart before it allows that to happen.

Corby edges an effective jab into the eye of one of the Skoogmelians, while I kick the legs out from under another and boot him across the dusty ground.

"We need to get back to the ship," I say. "Look, I'll distract them. You run for the stairway, get on board, and I'll see you there just as soon as I can get away."

"Not a chance. I'm not leaving a soft-skinned prince alone with these fuck-knuckles. You'll be torn limb from limb. And then the limbs will be mailed to your daddy, for money. You said yourself that's what would happen. Right? They know who you are. And it's even worse now we know your uncle's involved."

I don't answer, as I'm busy shoving one row of Skoogmelians into another. It causes a brief domino effect as a crowd of them topples all together to the ground.

"Here's what we'll do, then," she says, chopping one of them in the throat with the edge of her open palm. "You run for the ship and I'll distract them."

"Not in a million years. I am not leaving you alone with these aliens either." I punch one square in the nose.

"Oh, come on." She breaks off to spin around and kick her leg out to waist height, throwing another Skoogmelian off balance. There are still more heading our way all the time. Where the hell are they all coming from? "You know how to fly that super fancy ship. I know how to create a distraction. Let's play to our strengths, huh?"

I sigh irritably. "This is not at all proper. I cannot leave you alone with these monsters."

"Bullshit. It's only for a moment."

Weighing up the possibilities takes seconds. Corby does make a good point. She's probably better at doing something wild to command their attention, and I'm probably better at flying the ship. Only because I've had some practice with advanced vehicles, and she's used to flying some medieval tin can. Otherwise, I'm sure she'd whip my ass at flying too. But I cannot risk her life by waiting for her to make her own escape. I must modify the plan accordingly.

I won't wait for her on the ship. I'll fly back over here and drop down a rescue capsule for her.

"Take the gun," I say, pressing it into her hand. "I want you to know I think this is insane. I'm only going along with your idea because you're a career criminal who probably knows how to get out of a sticky situation. And I need to keep you safe. And if this is the way, then so be it."

"Career criminal? Fuck you, rich boy."

One of the Skoogmelians grabs Corby around the shoulders, and she knocks him off with the butt of the gun. That's probably all it's good for, now it won't fire any more.

"Okay. Fine. Do your thing, Corby Frayne."

I shift to my lion form. Sprinting to the ship gets me there almost immediately, but it still feels too long. I jump on board and fire up the ship's computer.

"Emergency capsule," I yell. "Prepare to unload, and reload with living cargo."

"Preparation under way," the computer-generated voice assures me.

I can't catch a glimpse of Corby on the viewing monitor because the angle of the external cameras is wrong. She's on the ground, and the cameras are designed to pick up information in space. The best thing I can do is just to fly back as fast as I can to the scene.

If I had to guess how long it took until we were hovering over the place where I had recently stood, I'd say hours. In reality, it must have been just a few moments. I ordered the ship's control system to drop down the capsule, and switched on the PA system, so I could talk to Corby outside.

"Get in," I shout. "Do it now."

At last, I can see Corby on the monitor. She has opened the capsule, and she's climbing inside. One of the Skoogmelians seems to put one of his tentacles inside just as she's closing the door. Mercilessly, she slams it shut and he squeals. He removes his crushed tentacle from the door and scuttles away.

"You inside the capsule?" I ask her.

"Mostly. Yeah."

"Mostly?"

"Just hoist me up, Your frickin' Highness. Get me back on that ship. What are you waiting for?"

I make it happen. In lion form, I am even stronger than I am on two legs. It takes seconds to retrieve the capsule.

When the capsule is fully inside the ship, I set the doors to close automatically and then jump down to help Corby out.

"Hey, furry guy. You know, I didn't exactly get away in one piece," Corby says, as she steps out of the capsule and pats my mane. Her voice sounds strange. My stomach lurches. I shift back immediately.

"What happened to you? Are you okay?" I hold her shoulders so I can study her at arm's length, and then turn her around, inspecting all over. I'm looking for lost body parts, wounds, or injuries of any kind. Somehow, I miss what the real issue is.

"So it's true. Guys really don't notice when a girl gets her hair done."

"What?"

She lifts her hair up in both hands, and I realize half of it is missing. The right side is as long and tangled as it was before. The left is now the length of her earlobe. I twist her around again so I can see where these two lengths meet in the back. There's a big slice taken out of her hair from the back, with the lengths now graduating from earlobe to below her shoulder in a sharp diagonal slash.

"What do you think?" She poses like a fashion model, pushing one hip out and making a goofy pouting expression. I know she's joking, but it stirs my blood.

"Did they cut your flesh?"

"Amazingly, no. I ducked as they slashed. Otherwise I think they might be holding my severed head, instead of just a bunch of hair." She shrugs. "I was lucky this time."

My heart bangs at double speed. Rage and protectiveness surge through me. "It is lucky for *them* that you are not hurt. I would shred them to molecules if they had hurt you."

She waves the thought away. "Nah, you're good. I'm pretty happy with my new look actually. Always meant to try out the asymmetric look. Now's my chance." She looks me up and down. "Back in your birthday suit, huh? Do me a favor, dude. Don't bother finding your clothes. I could use some eye candy right now."

Her flirtation is all the provocation I need. The thought of having nearly lost her is too much. I cannot hold back the urgent call of my lion.

Holding her hands, I push her backward, until she backs right up against the wall of the ship. I lean down, so our foreheads touch. Her hands are still in mine, and I pull them around my waist and leave them there.

"What are you doing?" she says, her eyes not leaving my mouth.

"This," I say. And then I kiss her, hard and unrelenting.

My hands slide across her back, one heading upward to hold the back of her butchered hair, and the other steadying her in the small of her back. She moves a little, sliding hand behind my head while the other grips onto my arm. Her fingernails dig into my bicep.

She's holding on to me for dear life.

My knee slides between hers. A tiny moan escapes her.

Our kiss become deeper and more passionate. Our tongues touch for a second, and I lift her right off her feet, turning us both around so I can move her onto the flight deck. I set her down next to the navigator screen, my hands lingering over the luscious curve of her ass.

"Jalton," she pants, as I kiss down her neck to her collarbone, pulling her shirt down so one smooth shoulder is exposed. "I don't know if we should—"

"We should. We must."

My tongue traces a line along her neck, and she moans again. "Oh my God, Jalton." Then all of a sudden she puts out a hand and pushes my head away. "Wait. We... Oh God. We can't."

I stop immediately. "What?"

"We just can't."

It kills me, but I pull away. "Okay. If you don't want this, I don't want this either."

"Oh, man. You *know* I want this." She lifts her legs up so they're around my waist and tugs me closer to her. But she's still holding my head so I can't kiss her. It's torture. Exquisite torture. "I just don't know if—"

There's a loud bleep on the ship's communication device. I stare at it, willing it to explode. Or disappear. Anything to stop it interrupting this moment.

It doesn't stop bleeping. It just keeps on.

"You'd better get that," she says, pulling her shirt back over her shoulder. She moves her legs away from me, and jumps off the flight desk.

Damn it. I glare at the communication device. Looks like the only thing that's going to explode around here is me.

Hitting the panel with unnecessary force, I shout "Yes?" in my own language. Even now, I can't take my eyes off my fiery girl. She fishes in the pocket of her uniform and pulls something out.

Deftly, she pulls her uneven hair up into a loose heap and fastens it with a band.

I'm so busy looking at Corby fixing her hair, I barely register that the person talking through the communication device is my uncle. *Again.*

At last, the fact hits my dumb blood-deprived brain.

"Uncle Mirodag?"

"What the hell are you doing on Skoogmel, Jalton?"

My hardness subsides quickly, as my critical faculties return. "What the...?"

"Answer me, boy. Did you finish the job as we agreed? Tell me you obeyed the order."

Rage pumps into my chest. I ball my fists. "I told you I'd *take care of this job.*"

"But you didn't, did you? Taking care of it is not the same as obeying orders. Stop avoiding the question. I don't want to hear any more of your slippery weasel words."

"Uncle, I hardly think the--"

"No. As I thought. You didn't do it." Uncle Mirodag can't hide the contempt in his voice. "You'd have thought that after an encounter with Kreapers, you'd think twice about crossing me."

It takes a moment for the ice in his voice to reach me. My brain tells me I've got it wrong, and that he can't be telling me what I think he is. But deep down, I already knew from our last call. He just confirmed what I suspected.

"You're tracking us?"

"Do you think I'm an idiot? Of course I'm tracking you."

"You sent *Kreapers*?" The growl in my voice makes Corby freeze. "What kind of person sends Kreapers to their nephew? You're my father's brother. What the *fuck* do you think he'd do if he heard about this?"

"You idiotic boy. You really think your father would care? He's as disgusted as the rest of us with your behavior."

I don't believe Uncle Mirodag, not completely. But his words have an effect. They were intended to. Is it likely my father's knee-deep in the swamp of corruption, just like Uncle Mirodag is? Is that possible?

If I help Corby to expose the corruption, am I signing my own father's death warrant?

"You're a damn fool, Jalton," my uncle says. "You'll pay for this mistake. You'll pay, and pay. And your little friend will be the downpayment." He curses under his breath. "My compliments on her new haircut. Tell her next time the blade will not miss."

The communication device goes dead.

I pick it up and hurl it across the room. It hits the wall and splinters into tiny pieces.

"Bastard," I snarl at the fragments.

Corby's hand covers her mouth and her eyes are wide. I'm right in front of her, holding her, before I even register that I've moved.

"You need to tell me more of what you know about my family," I say. "And I need to see what's on that chip."

"Why? How would it help? It would only freak you out."

"I need to know," I say, suddenly calm, "because we're going to do something about it. We're going to cut out the rotten heart of the Imperial Order. We're going to stop the killing, and the lies. We're going to do right by your family. And we're going to make things right. Just the way they should be."

She blinks. "We are?"

"We are. Me, you, and that damn chip. Where are you supposed to take it?"

"Quintagon. I have a contact waiting for my arrival. If he hasn't given up on me, that is."

"Who could ever give up on you? I steal a kiss. She smiles and presses her fingers into my biceps, gazing up at me with desire. I can't wait to follow up on the promise of that look.

I tap the voice activation panel and speak to the ship's computer system. "Navigate the ship to Quintagon. Commander Frayne will direct us from there."

The flight to Quintagon takes about eighteen Earth hours. In that time, Jalton managed to eat another two meals, and I caught a quick nap.

I wake up feeling scuzzy. It's been a while since my last wash and change of clothes.

"Do we have a shower on board this ship?" I ask. It's silly, because I know it's very unlikely. This ship is small, even if it is a masterpiece of futuristic technology. So it blows me away when Jalton says "Sure," and directs me to a door in the back corner.

"That's a shower?"

"It's a kind of shower."

I look at him. "A *kind* of shower? Why is that suddenly less appealing?"

"I don't know. You tell me."

"It's definitely a human-style shower? With hot

water and soap and a towel to dry yourself at the end of it?"

He thinks about this for a minute. "I'm not sure if you'd describe it as '*human style*'."

This just concerns me even more. I watch him quizzically, as he throws the last few morsels of food into his mouth and chews them.

"You're sure it sprays water, Jalton? You're not sending me into a hydrochloric acid bath, meant for some other alien species with skin that can withstand the harshest chemicals?"

"No!"

"Well, all right then."

I stroll off toward the door. Looking back at him, I sigh. He'd better not be playing guessing games. If this shower hurts me, I'm going to lose my shit.

As it turns out, he's right. Behind the door is a small square-floored room. The walls and ceiling are smooth all around, but it has a textured tile underfoot so you don't slip and land on your butt. To the side is a metal bench, shaped a little like a human shower stall, except for one important detail. There's no drainage hole for the water to escape.

"Details," I mutter to myself. These Imperial Order guys think of everything, so it's going to be fine.

I'm not sure how any of the controls work, so I

strip my clothes off in blind faith, and throw them onto the bench. It's still impossible to understand the practicalities of this shower stall. Stepping carefully into the center of the square, I look around the ceiling. Nothing. No shower head and no drainage. This is the weirdest freaking shower I ever saw.

"Water?" I say into the air, randomly.

And lo and behold, water appears. It flows from the ceiling, heated to exactly the right temperature. Damn. This alien technology is good stuff. Apparently the central command system can understand English too, just like Jalton does.

"Shampoo", I say, hoping it knows what I mean. It does. A glass oval appears from what seems like nowhere, and I hold out my hand. It dispenses a blob of creamy lilac shampoo into my palm. It smells like heaven.

I wash my hair and rinse it, and then I ask for conditioner, not quite believing it'll work. But it does. I request shower gel, and sure enough, it is given. These little glass ovals just appear when I call.

It might be the technology, or it might be because I was super dirty, but this is the best shower I've ever had. Truly. It's blissful.

When I'm clean and rinsed all over, I linger in the spray, turning around. The water feels so good, it's like a warm hug. And now there is a drainage outlet after all. It must have appeared when I switched on the spray.

It's not quite as great as the real life warm hug I got from the mysterious prince on the other side of the door, but it's good. It's all good.

Eventually, I decide it's probably time to stop showering. I turn it off just by asking it to stop, and then I stand there in confusion. There are no towels. There are no shelves, or anything. It's a blank room.

Fortunately, I only waste about a minute contemplating this error. All around me, fans start to whirr. I feel a warm, thick, buttersoft breeze skirt all over my body at various intervals. I'm dry in about a minute.

"Nice," I say, to absolutely no one.

I'm standing in the middle of the room, enjoying the caress of the warm air against my tired back muscles, when I remember I don't have any clean clothes. I'm going to have to put my old outfit on again. That sucks, because I'm all clean, and it isn't. Ew.

"Wish you had a clean outfit for me, magic shower," I mutter, as I reach for my heap of crumpled clothing.

There's a rush of air again. I'm just about knocked clean off my feet when I notice a small box emerge from the floor and dangle in mid-air.

"What the...?" I reach tentatively for the box. It

opens the second my fingers reach it. Inside, there's a neat stack of folded fabric. I touch it, my mouth falling open.

"Seriously? There's an automatic clothes thing in this place too?"

I grab hold of the fabric and shake it out. It's a one-piece pantsuit thing, made of some super-soft stretchy stuff. Kind of a onesie, I guess. And it's going to hug every curve.

There's underwear in the box too, made of something silky. I slip everything on, and laugh out loud when the onesie fastens itself without any help. It fits perfectly.

Resting my hands on my hips, I look down. It's tight, but in a good way. Maybe I'm kidding myself, but I feel like I look pretty badass in this. Like a superhero.

"Guess a mirror is too much to ask for?" I call out.

Nothing appears, but I don't mind. I'm going to wear it anyway. Beats the grimy stuff I had on earlier.

I run my hands through my hair. It's not even tangled. Usually, I have to deep condition my hair for hours, and comb it really gently. Whatever those hair products were, I want to take a stack of them home with me when I leave.

When I return to the flight deck, Jalton is taking a call with someone. They're talking in his own language. It's a nice sound. Kind of lilting, but with a scratchy gruffness to it. Wonder how hard it is to learn it? Probably super hard. Imperial Order royals grew up around it, so it's easy for them.

Jalton turns to see me come in, and looks away. Then he double-takes and stares back at me. His eyes slide down my new outfit to my feet, then slowly up again until they reach my eyes. There's a fire in his eyes that makes me shiver.

He doesn't speak for a few moments. Finally, he mutters a few curt words, as though he's ending the call. Then he stands, and approaches me.

My breathing speeds up and my limbs tingle. He's so tall. So big, and so very tall. I don't even realize I'm doing it at first, but I somehow edge backward so I'm leaning against the wall of the ship. I'm plastered against a bank of environmental monitoring screens.

He takes both my hands and looms over me. "You smell incredible."

"Uh... thank you?"

"You look..." He looks down at me again, with hunger in his eyes. I lick my lips. Desire courses through me. I shift from foot to foot, hot under the sun-like heat of his stare.

What's he going to do? My imagination is in overdrive, even though I'm trying to keep my cool.

He drops one of my hands and strokes my cheek with the back of his fingers.

"We must get to Quintagon. When you have taken the chip where it needs to go, we will arrange for a copy of all the evidence to go to my personal encrypted account. I will take it to my father."

"Your father?" I swallow, unable to take my eyes off his delicious mouth. "But what if he's involved in the bad stuff too?"

"My father does not concern himself with the running of his empire. If only he did. Perhaps the galaxies could have avoided all that misery."

He pulls my hand around his waist and moves in closer. Warmth pulses through me.

"So you think he'll want to take out the bad apples in the Imperial Order?" My voice sounds like a bird squawking. I'm so consumed with physical longing, I can hardly get my stupid brain to work.

"He will." Jalton threads his fingers into my freshly-washed hair and lifts up a handful. Then he bends to my neck and inhales, from my shoulder to my ear. It'd be weird if anyone else did it, but when it's a seven-foot lion shifter who also looks a lot like a Greek god, it's just ridiculously hot.

"That's... oh good then, that's good," I babble, tipping my head back. I close my eyes as he begins to kiss my throat, up to my cheeks and then finally my lips.

It feels like we've been waiting so long for this moment, even though we only met yesterday. Is it yesterday? In Earth time, it'd be a day ago. Out here in space, it's impossible to keep track. Either way, it's like he's a tall glass of iced water and I've been in the desert for hours.

We kiss passionately as my hands roam over his thick, hard muscles. He's so big, I can barely get a grip on his arms. As he pulls me in closer, I feel his hardness jutting into me. I can't help but push back against him. He feels so good against me.

The only problem with wearing a badass super-hero onesie is that it's kind of inconvenient to remove in a hurry. I begin to wonder how exactly I'm going to get out of it. Suddenly, getting out of it seems urgent.

"You are mine now," he growls into my hair. "You know that, Earth girl? Mine."

The raw animal lust in his voice makes me quiver. "I am?" I whisper, as he kisses me again.

"Fated mates. That's what we are." He lifts me effortlessly in one big arm so we're eye to eye.

"Fated mates?" I put out a hand to pause him. "Wait a second. Fated mates? That's a shifter thing. I'm not a shifter. I can't be anyone's fated mate."

He frowns, as though I'm cracking a joke that isn't very funny and he can't work out why. "Of course you are. This isn't an accident. Fate brought us together."

"Oh, come on. You believe that?" I'm being

lighthearted, but then I realize he isn't. He's deadly serious.

He sets me down on the floor, still holding me. "You *don't* believe in fate?"

I think about it. I think about how my family were bombed and my entire home town was erased from the map, just randomly, on the whim of some general on another planet. "Honestly? Not really. No."

"Then how do you explain the cascade of extraordinary events that led us together? Why are we both here, right now?"

"I believe a bunch of weird shit happens, and we all have to make the best of it from that point on."

He stares at me. Then his hands leave me. I want to shout "No, hold me again," but I don't.

"Royal shifters always have a fated mate. Usually it is somebody chosen by their parents. I have always known the woman chosen for me by my father was not my fated mate. I am equally sure now that it is you."

"Wow."

I can't think of anything else to say. He caught me off-guard with the fate stuff. My tongue is totally tied.

Now everything is a little awkward. I feel like I've said the wrong thing, or offended him in some way.

He smiles as he steps back, but it's a slightly sad smile. "No matter. We can talk about this some other time. Let's concentrate on getting to Quintagon as fast as we can." He sits at the flight desk and opens the navigation starcharts.

I stand on the spot, not sure what to do. Looks like somehow I blew it. Damn it.

And a quiet, pensive part of me wonders if there's something to it. Maybe fate is a thing. Maybe that explains why I ended up with Prince Jalton, instead of a regular prisoner inspector. If I had been processed by anyone else, I'd be dead by now.

If Prince Jalton hadn't taken a bet with his brother and ended up working with prisoners for one day, I wouldn't be here to even think about it.

A chill wafts across me. Holy shit. Maybe fate is a thing. Maybe that's what this is.

"Let me know if there's anything I can help with," I say, sitting next to my big handsome prince. "You know, with the flight to Quintagon and stuff."

He catches my eye and smiles. My heart flips over.

Mine. I like the sound of it.

The rest of the flight is good-humored and peaceful. There's still an undercurrent of awkwardness though. I feel so drawn to this alien prince, while also knowing he is totally unobtainable. The idea that we are fated mates blew my mind. I just couldn't deal with it. Now I feel silly.

But he's right, we do need to concentrate on our mission. If we don't get to Quintagon before Jalton's bad uncle works out where we're headed, it's all over. I'll be killed immediately. Jalton will be... actually, what would happen to him?

"What would your uncle do to you if he caught you? I mean, now you know he knows you know. Kinda thing."

Jalton leans back in his chair and swivels around toward me. "He'd kill me, of course."

I open my eyes wide. "Kill you? He'd kill his own flesh and blood?"

"Of course. I openly defied him. I absconded with a prisoner, and I refused a direct order from a senior royal. There's only one way out of that mess, and it's in a body bag."

He turns back to the navigation controls.

"Wow. You don't look too concerned about this."

"You think I should be quaking in my boots?"

"No, but..." I struggle to get the words out right. "You're risking your life for me. That's kind of a big deal."

"It's also a pretty big deal to meet your--" He doesn't finish the sentence. "We're near Quintagon now. See the green glow in the corner of the screen?" I turn my chair and peer over his shoulder. "That's Quintagon."

"Oh wow. That's near." A rush of relief washes over me. Perhaps we will make it after all.

"Is the person who needs the chip living in a major city?" Jalton asks.

"He's just outside the capital. If we land somewhere in the Porglissimo region, I can contact him from there."

"That'll work." He speaks the location command aloud, and the ship's computer confirms our path. It's a very businesslike voice. I prefer the varied tones of my Neela, and even though I know she's only an artificial voice, I kind of miss her.

We land in a quiet part of the Porglissimo district on Quintagon. It's a place where a lot of trade ships come and go, so we're able to enter without too much fuss. I speak to the transit supervisor as soon as we get there.

"Tollajif asked us to come," I say in a low voice. The supervisor nods. He's part of the Resistance too. Most transit workers are.

"Go right through. No need for paperwork. I'll sign that you're an authorized entrant."

"Thank you," I say, giving the customary Quintagonian bow. He returns it. Jalton copies the gesture, and the two of us walk through the gates like we're just a pair of regular traders.

"Will I be recognized here?" Jalton asks, looking around discreetly.

"Well, I don't know. Let's see. You're still wearing a uniform. Is that something people will associate with the Imperial Order royal family?"

"No, this is a prison inspection shifter's uniform."

"Then you're golden. People will just think you work for the big guys."

We keep walking, until I reach a public call interface. It's a silver pole with a pink spotted rectangle on it. Perfect for intergalactic visitors who might not have the right calling plan to use their cellphones on this world.

I say the codewords and add "Tollajif". Turning to Jalton, I whisper "That's the local name for our contact. He has a codename in the Resistance, but his real name is Tollajif. If anybody asks, we're delivering a consignment to him later this month and we're just checking his storage facilities."

"Got it."

There's a crackle of static and then Tollajif's voice rings out of the pole.

"Don't say my name," I warn him immediately in a low voice. Then I speak at a normal volume. "Tollajif, we're just checking your storage capacity for the consignment. We need to ensure you have the correct facilities available. May we meet with you today?"

"Absolutely," Tollajif says, with a smile in his voice. "Please wait for me at the traders' canteen and I'll take you to my storage unit."

Nervousness prickles across my skin. We're pretty safe here on Quintagon, I reason, because surely Jalton's uncle would have caught us before we got here? But I can't help but feel concerned.

Jalton still looks too tall, handsome and regal to be a trader, but he's doing his best not to stand out.

He keeps his eyes low and somehow manages to pass as a normal person.

"Don't shift," I warn him. "Not even if someone annoys you."

"Of course not. I'm not an idiot."

"Okay. Just making sure."

At the traders' canteen, we pick at a bowl of tasteless rice and edible flowers, and some kind of protein. I suspect it's probably bugs of some kind. Maybe crickets. There's a crunch and a spiciness which is just about bearable, but I'm not that hungry. I just want to get this transaction done. We still have the return journey to make. If Tollajif has distributed the material by then, the entire galaxy is going to be watching the story unfold. The chances of us arriving on Jalton's home planet quietly will be approximately zero.

At last, Tollajif arrives. He slides into the seat next to Jalton. He's about half Jalton's height, with cropped dark red hair and olive green skin. The color combination really works for him.

"You did not tell me you would have company," Tollajif says, looking through narrowed eyes at Jalton, and then back at me.

"Ah, yes. My colleague is an essential part of this job. I trust you don't mind my bringing him?"

Tollajif nods deeply. "If he is essential to your side of the operation, then I am content."

We make small talk for a few minutes, so

nobody watching us will be suspicious. Then, as casually as possible, I rest my boot on my knee. Tollajif reads the signs and smiles.

"I'm so happy you could make it here for the trade," he says.

"Me too." I start talking about anything and nothing, just filling the air with pointless chatter, while I very carefully open my boot's secret compartment. Reaching under the table, I slide out the chip.

"Well, I am reassured that you have the correct storage facilities for our consignment. Perhaps you could show us those on our next visit."

"I would be honored," Tollajif says. We all stand and bow. Jalton looks at me pointedly. I wink at him.

"Oh yes," I add. "Tollajif, would you also please send a copy of the data you have to this account?" Jalton tells Tollajif the address, and Tollajif closes his eyes for a moment. Then he bows. "It is memorized. I will send the copy now, from the transmitter in my personal vehicle."

"Perfect."

"And allow me to bid you farewell in the traditional Earth manner," Tollajif adds, and holds out a hand. I take his and shake it, and we bow again. The chip transfers seamlessly from my palm to his during the handshake.

"I will be in touch," Tollajif says, and smiles broadly. Then he walks away, with the precious cargo I risked my life to bring here.

Relief floods over me. I feel like I'm lying down in the surf, letting the warm tropical ocean glide over me and float me away. "We did it," I whisper.

"May I take you home now?" Jalton says. "My home planet is many vaylons from here. I want to get you back safely as quickly as we can. I'm going to look out for a wormhole to speed up the journey."

"Sounds good," I say, unable to stop myself grinning like a crazy Cheshire cat. The nerves have been replaced by exhilaration.

We did it. We got the chip to Tollajif. We're going to bring down the Imperial Order. Or, at least, the part of it that's corrupt.

I can't even imagine how living in the galaxy will feel without the fist of the Imperial Order being slammed into our faces all the time, but it'll be awesome to find out.

"You think Tollajif will send the file as quickly as he suggested?" Jalton asks, as we thread our way through the crowds. We're walking slowly, because rushing back to the vehicle will set off an automatic transit gate inspection. We've got this far and we don't want to spoil it now.

"I expect so," I say. "He's a man of his word."

Jalton appears thoughtful. "And he will spread the information through his network?"

"Now he has hard evidence, he'll spread it everywhere. Every intergalactic news source. All over the cosmonet. The news media wouldn't touch the story if there wasn't any evidence. Everyone talks about Imperial Order brutality all the time on a personal level, but there's never any way to prove it. But now there is. Dates, places, names, photographs, even videos. They're all on that chip."

Jalton is quiet for a moment. I start to worry.

"Wait a second," I say. "You're not starting to regret doing this are you? I mean, because it's your family..." I trail off.

He stops and faces me, taking both my hands. "Are you kidding? Of course I don't regret it. What I regret is not knowing about any of this before I met you. I should have been working to change things from the day I came of age. I regret taking no interest in politics, like my father. We're just a bunch of spoiled rich boys living in luxury, wasting our time and doing nothing to earn our lavish lifestyles."

"Well, if you put it like that--" I smile. "Nah. Come on. You're okay, dude. You're a good guy. Take me home now."

"I thought you'd never ask," he says, with a sexy smile that basically melts my panties right under my stretchy superhero onesie.

We're nearly at the transit gate now, so we slow down even more to an idle saunter. Traders are usually lazy and like to stretch out their assignments, to make sure they don't get sent on any extras. Jalton follows my lead, and we joke together while we amble along.

The gate is within touching distance when suddenly I feel a hand on my shoulder. I turn to look behind me.

"Commander Corby Frayne, you are under arrest."

My hands are torn roughly behind me and clipped together.

Jalton hits the people handcuffing me, and they fall backward. But then something terrible happens. Someone shoots Jalton with a stun gun. I scream. He drops to his knees, his eyes only partly open now.

"What the hell are you doing?" I shriek over my shoulder.

"You've gone too far this time, Wildcat," my captor says. His voice is a menacing sneer. "And you even dragged a royal into the gutter with you. That'll count against you when you appear before the Imperial Court."

"Who are you?"

"We are enforcers," he says. "And you don't have such a smart mouth now, I notice. That's good. That's just as it should be. I have questions to ask you. And you're going to answer them."

"Why would I talk to you?"

"Because every time you talk back to me, or refuse to answer, or do anything at all I don't like, I have official permission to do this."

And then he hits me. Right across the face. I gasp in shock, tasting blood.

Jalton roars, even though he's not in his lion form, and grabs the enforcer's leg. He yanks him down onto the floor, aiming a heavy punch at his face.

Right before Jalton's fist can connect, he's shot with the stream of the stun gun again. Only this time there are three more enforcers with guns, all shooting him it at once. Not even a royal lion shifter can withstand that.

Jalton drops back to the floor. There's a flash of angry lion across his face, and then it's gone. He sinks down, unconscious.

"No!" I screech.

Kicking and yelling, I'm dragged into the back of some kind of road vehicle. There are no windows and it's hot and airless.

As I stumble backward with my hands bound, I fall over something on the floor.

It's Tollajif's lifeless body.

My friend and colleague lies beside me, staring up at nothing.

I scream.

Then the doors slam, and I'm left alone with poor Tollajif in the darkness.

My lion roars inside me. How it would love to swipe the insolence off their faces with one mighty paw.

"Oh, come now, Your Highness." The man opposite me almost drops his gun, he's so amused. His mocking tone makes me want to tear him limb from limb. "Who do you think arranged all of this?" He gestures to the rest of his crew with one open hand. "Your family knows what it wants. As always."

"You're telling me my own family wanted me to be shot with a stun gun?" I laugh back at him, with scorn in my voice. "Hardly."

"Who else? Hit squads cost money. Your uncle has plenty."

My lion goes crazy inside. "My uncle? I presume you mean Mirodag?"

"That's the guy. Great boss. Actually, he's not such a great boss. But we know what's best for us. Your uncle wanted Corby removed, and he wanted you brought to your senses. And here we are. The right men for the job. Ready, willing and able."

They all laugh again, and my inner lion just about explodes with righteous fury.

"Is my uncle here?" I clench my fists, ice shooting down my spine. "Bring him to me."

"It's not for you to issue orders, Your Highness," the leader says, even more pointedly than before. "Not any more. But you shall have your wish. Your uncle wants you brought to him when he arrives. He should be here soon."

The room we are in is comfortable, and I am not shackled. But six men stand over me with guns. And this time they aren't just for immobilization. These are real lethal weapons. By the sound of it, they would not hesitate to use them.

Violence would be good right now. My lion wants me to inflict violence. It wants to shred these fools and go rescue Corby Frayne.

But my rational side knows that is not the right way. Even if I did manage to break out of here and find Corby, there will be another layer of security with guns. And another. And another. We will never be free of my uncle's many tentacles if we simply try to run.

I'm going to have to play my uncle's game more cleverly than that.

"Fine," I say, sinking back onto my bench. "Okay. You win. I'll see him. Let me know when he's here." I rest my head on the wall behind the bench and close my eyes, as though I'm catching up on a nap.

The men think they have won somehow, because I appear to be backing down. After a few snickers and catcalls, they begin to talk among themselves and leave me alone.

But I am not asleep. I am listening to every word they say, and planning my next move.

One way or another, I am getting out of here. And I am taking Corby with me.

⁂

"You always were an easily-led milquetoast, Jalton," Uncle Mirodag says, when he arrives. He lifts his chin and peers disapprovingly at me down his nose.

I need to get my furious inner lion under control. So I promise it a treat later if it behaves itself now. The anger still courses around my body, but I manage to restrain my urge to shift. If that bastard can keep his animal in check, so can I.

"I don't understand why you're going to all this trouble just for one little Wildcat," I say, wiping a drip from the cup in front of me. "It's almost as though you have something to hide. Something the Wildcat could reveal, if you're not careful."

His face is as cool and emotionless as ever. "The girl is a criminal. A thief, a traitor, and a liar. You should be careful, Jalton. You can tell a lot about a person by the company they keep."

"Very true."

We stare each other down for a while. Eventually, I break the silence.

"So what now? How does this end? What is it you're planning to do with the girl, and with me?"

Uncle Mirodag takes a deep breath and smooths down his robe. "The girl is currently being put to use. And you? Well, that depends."

"Put to use?" I say sharply.

Uncle Mirodag leans forward. "Don't tell me you have feelings for the urchin?"

I keep my expression neutral. "It brings the Imperial Order into disrepute if its prisoners are treated badly."

"Oh, come now, Jalton. Nobody in the galaxy gives a fig if prisoners are treated badly. They should not have committed crime if they did not wish to be punished for it."

"What are you doing with the girl?"

"As I say, she is being put to use. She will be a welcome addition to the managerial hostess chalet. She's not fit to serve as a companion to higher-born noblemen, of course. But her charms will suffice for the middle ranking officials."

My blood runs cold. My lion is just about ready to start a fucking war. Beautiful, fragrant Corby is not being bought and sold as a companion. Not while I still draw breath.

But I have to remember my uncle holds all the aces here. I am in no position to change things, unless I do so wisely.

I remember the game with my brother and Kaljo. It was so recent, and yet it feels so long ago. If I had not agreed to Reago's bet, I would not be in this position.

But then Corby Frayne would be dead. And so all this must be down to Fate. It must be.

Fate demands that I handle this with finesse and subtlety. I will not disappoint Fate.

"Then we have a problem, Uncle." I lean back, legs wide apart, arms resting on the back of the bench. "Corby Frayne is to be *my* companion. I say she is fit to serve me. I may consider releasing her to the criminal justice system once I have had my fill of her. But for now, she is reserved. There is a virtual sign around her neck, with my name on it."

It makes me feel sick to speak of my beautiful girl like this, but I must win her freedom by any means necessary. For now, this is the only way.

"You wish to use the girl yourself?"

"Naturally. Why on earth do you think I

abducted her from the prison cell in the first place?"
I laugh heartily.

"You accompanied her to the handing over of Imperial Order secrets. That was no accident."

"That chip was worthless, Uncle. Do you think I would have let the recipient get away, if it had not been?" I know I'm pushing my luck with this line.

"It does not matter anyway," Uncle Mirodag says, shrugging. "The Resistance member named Tollajif is dead. We tidied up the fallout from your messy handiwork, Jalton."

Tollajif is dead?

Guilt and bile rise in my throat. I should have done something to stop this. I should have gone to my father before my uncle went completely insane with power.

"I'm going to need Corby Frayne returned to me," I say, keeping my voice light with supreme effort.

There's a glint in my uncle's eye. He is a sadistic man, who loves to watch people suffer. I imagine he will do his very best to torture me about Corby, for as long as he can. And I can take it. Just so long as he leaves her the hell alone.

"What's it worth to you, oh beloved nephew?"

"What do you mean?"

"Well, now. It's obviously important to you to get sexual favors from this Earth harpy. What will you give me if I allow you an intimate visit?"

"I'm not asking for an *intimate visit*. I'm *telling* you I'm taking her away with me."

"*Telling*. Interesting choice of word." Uncle Mirodag rubs his pointed chin and regards me through narrowed eyes. "I am prepared to allow you time with the prisoner. On two conditions."

"Name them." How my lion longs to throw him across the room.

"One. You dispose of her when you have finished, or pass her back to my team to do the dirty work if you aren't up to it."

My lion is on the very edge of breaking free. I will it to stay contained, for just a while longer. "And two?"

"Two is that you forget you ever heard of that chip. It never happened. You didn't meet the traitors, you never came her to Quintagon, and you never heard of any controversy surrounding our family. Is that clear?"

"I hear you," I say. "But I'm not sure about your plan. There might be a better way we can negotiate this."

Uncle Mirodag looks taken aback. "Such as?"

I lean back in my chair and shoot him an arrogant grin.

"We play a game. If I win, I get to do whatever I like with the girl. Including taking her away with me as my travel companion. If you win, you can do as you wish with us both. Winner takes all."

My uncle's eyes dart to the ceiling. He's thinking about what I just said.

"Of course, if you're not confident in your card skills, I can understand you might wish to go back to the old-fashioned coercion method," I add.

The prod works. He shakes his head in irritation.

"Jalton, your card skills are hopeless. You're the world's worst bluffer. You don't know one end of a card from the other. And, from what your brother told me, you're only here because you screwed up a game spectacularly. This is probably the stupidest idea you've ever had, and that's saying something."

I smile briefly. He's right. In the past, I've always been terrible at keeping a poker face. Like with Reago the other night.

I'm just going to have to smash it out of the park this time around.

"Then what are you waiting for, Uncle? Do your worst. Show me who's boss."

Uncle Mirodag guffaws, slapping his thighs in hilarity. "You are seriously challenging me to a game of cards, and you wish the criminal's entire future to hang upon it?"

"That's what I said."

He can barely contain his mirth. "You'd pin the survival of a crook on a card game? Even though you are the family's most hapless player, and your little pet thief deserves what's coming to her?"

I stretch both arms wide, in a gesture of open frankness. "Humor me. Life as a prince is boring. Nothing much ever happens. This is the most fun I've had in a long time. Give me the chance of some practice at playing cards, and I'll try to improve. And we may as well make the stakes high. That way, we really have something to play for."

Uncle Mirodag smiles unpleasantly. "Okay. Here's what we'll do. We'll play the game, as you suggest. But it really will be winner takes all. If you win, you get to leave with the girl. I won't follow you. You can do what you will with her. Consider her your personal slave."

"And if you win?"

"You kill the girl yourself, right in front of me and my team. We then take you home to your father and tell him everything. A very limited version of everything. And if you utter a word of any of this to the family, we will torture you until you confess that you are responsible for all the—" —he makes a face—"corruption in our otherwise pure and noble empire."

I clench the muscles of my jaw. "You'll stick to our agreement? If I win, you'll hand her over without complaint?"

"Of course."

"Then, Uncle Mirodag," I say, preparing to bow deeply in the usual royal way. "You have yourself a deal."

"It is a pleasure negotiating with you, nephew," he says, clapping me on the back. "Good idea about the game, too. Lateral thinking. I like it. There may be hope for you yet."

I crack my knuckles and think about all the ways in which I'm going to make him pay for what he's done.

"Then let us play," I say.

The cuffs around my wrist are starting to dig into my skin. I can't get my hands close enough together to rub them, so I have to just ignore the soreness.

"You'll be prepared for the first offering soon," a bored female voice says from somewhere behind me. I try to turn, but the chains attaching my arms and legs to the wall are too short.

She walks into my line of vision at last, and sits on a stool, holding what looks like a tablet notebook and a stylus. She looks like she's from Quintagon, with the usual olive green skin, but her hair is a bright aqua blue. It's not a good color combination.

"There's a small change of plan," she drones, "but I don't need to run that past you unless you're really interested."

"Change of plan?" It's hot in here. A trickle of sweat slides down my back, inside my onesie. I'm still wearing it, but now there's a rip across the thigh. "I don't even know what the original plan was."

"Didn't they tell you?" The female Quintagonian looks mildly surprised. "I suppose they thought there was no point. Okay, well here's what's happening. From now on, you're going to be based here, as a companion. Your work will mostly be servicing managerial level Imperial Order officials. Possibly the occasional junior doctor or lawyer. It depends on demand, and how many girls we have left at any one time."

"Companion?" I scoot up, trying to relieve the numbness in my butt. "You mean... a hooker?"

"We prefer to say companion." She scrolls through the screen on her tablet. "Now, let me get the details right... oh yes. Prince Jalton is now playing cards with his uncle, and they'll decide your fate that way."

Jalton is okay. I'm so grateful, I almost forget the rest of what she said. Then it percolates through my brain.

"Decide my fate?" I say.

She doesn't elaborate.

I persist. "How do you mean?"

She sighs heavily, as though supervising me is awfully inconvenient. "You're the stake in a game of cards, Frayne. They've been playing for some time. If Prince Jalton loses, he has to kill you himself. If he wins, he'll use you as his personal companion for a while, and then presumably he'll kill you later. Or hand you back to be killed."

I give this a moment to sink in, and then I clear my throat. "Uh, ma'am? Are you saying that either way I'm going to be killed?"

"Obviously," she says, in an acid tone. "You're a criminal. What exactly were you expecting?"

She finishes whatever she's doing on her tablet, and then leaves the room without another word. I squirm again, desperately trying to find a position that doesn't hurt my wrists, my ankles, or my butt. It's almost impossible.

So Jalton's playing a card game with me as the prize, or punishment? Holy fuck. Is he for real? Is there any way this isn't as bad as it sounds? I run the facts over in my mind.

Jalton told me he was awful at card games, which is why he lost and had to process prisoners. But what does it matter? Either way, I'm history.

I'm wallowing in self-pity when the door flies open again. A team of armed guards stands in the doorway.

"Get up, Frayne," the front guard says. "You're required."

I stand up, with difficulty. One of the men unlocks my shackles so I can walk. My hands are still bound together behind me. On trembling legs, I follow behind him. Guns are pointed at me from all sides. It's not like I stand a chance of fighting, or running away, so it's definitely overkill.

We walk for a long time, down endless corridors that remind me of a maze. I half expect us to end up right back where we started. But eventually we reach the end of a dark walkway, and stop outside a heavy gray door. The leader guard opens it and stands in front of it, clearing a path through.

"In here," he says, shoving me through the doorway.

I almost trip, and can't steady myself because of my shackled hands. Will this be my first client? The horror of it hits me deep in the gut.

But then I look up, and my breath catches in my throat.

Jalton is sitting there, playing cards. He has what looks like a cocktail in front of him, and he's sitting comfortably in a reclining wing-backed chair, clutching his cards high and close, so nobody can see them.

"Hello, Commander Frayne," he says, with a wink.

I can't tell how well the game is going. I'm not even sure what outcome I should be hoping for. Apparently I'm in trouble, either way. Big execution-level trouble. What difference does it make if I'm killed now or later? The whole situation feels hopeless.

I'm holding out hope that Jalton is going to pull a trick out of the bag and save us both. But looking at him now, I'm not so sure.

He's back in his regal robes. The uniform is long gone. Of course, he looks hot as hell in royal clothing too.

I'm pretty bummed we never got the chance to finish what we started back on the ship. I guess now we never will. Unless he wins the game, and then I'm his prize for some brief time, and then... Yeah, I'm not doing that. I'm not a damn concubine. He missed his chance.

I ache for his touch, just as much as I curse the stupid circumstances that brought us together.

The asshole Mirodag smirks at me, then back at Jalton. "Your wench admires your robes, Jalton. She finds you most pleasing in your finery."

Jalton does not look up at either me or his uncle. He selects a card out of his own hand, with a look of intense concentration, and lays it on the table. "Your turn, Uncle."

Mirodag matches the move, and continues to leer at me. "She's quite a beauty, Jalton. I can see why you wanted to try her on for size."

A muscle in Jalton's shoulder twitches, but he does not respond. I'm angry that he doesn't speak up to defend me. But I guess maybe he really is just a royal prick after all.

The memory of his kisses flies back into my stupid brain. I lick my lips, remembering how good he felt. And how good he smelled. And how strong his arms were as they lifted me onto his lap. And...

But there's no point dwelling on all that. None of that is real any more. It's all in the past now.

And I have no future. Not with Jalton, and not on my own.

The only way I'm getting off this planet is in a casket.

I'm royally screwed.

I glance over my cards with quick flicks of the eye, as though they're mediocre. I don't stare at them in disbelief. I don't gaze at them in excitement. I don't move a muscle, except to sip my drink every now and then. And I'm fake-drinking that.

When they bring in Corby Frayne, my muscles feel like they're tightening to the point of pain. It takes a lot of effort to make them relax. If I let my mask slip, I'll lose the game. My uncle is a great game player, and he's known me since I was a child. If anyone can see through my bluffing, it's him.

That's why I have to work my ass off to make sure my bluff is bulletproof.

My cards are incredible. Truly great cards. I've never had such a good hand. But if I let that information out, my uncle will start to play defensively. I could still lose, even with these cards. It'd take some doing, but I'm confident my uncle is enough of an asshole to try.

So I plan to stay neutral and non-committal, right up until the last part of the game. Then I'll start making it look like I have terrible cards, and I was just trying to cover it up before. I'll look jaded and disappointed.

This has to work. There is no plan B.

Corby is pushed onto a chair a short distance from my uncle and me. I hear the scraping of the chair on the floor, and the little exclamation as her luscious behind hits the seat. My lion growls inside me with desire.

I don't turn to look at her, at first. I just feel the warmth of her presence. Then I wink at her. I have to be a royal asshole right now.

If there's a way to reassure someone silently that you've got this and it's going to be okay, I'd like to know it. She must be terrified. I cannot take her in my arms and make it all right, not yet.

But I will make it up to her once we are free. I will move the heavens and the stars to make it so.

"Your turn to deal," drawls my uncle. He has had one too many of the mauve cocktails he insists on drinking. I have deliberately not drunk mine. My head is clear.

"Sure, sorry," I say. I'm acting the hapless amateur, pretending I have no idea about whose turn it is. Like I'm not watching this game like the predator I really am inside. I failed against Reago because I was lazy and didn't bother. This time, I'm working hard.

I'm analysing everything. With clumsy mannerisms, I deal the cards between us, and put the remainder on a loose pile between us.

My uncle must be in a hurry. He keeps glancing at the time, which is projected on the wall to our right. He needs to be somewhere. I could use this to my advantage.

For only the second time since she was brought in, I allow myself to steal a glance at Corby Frayne. She is a picture of glowing beauty, gracing the old bench with her luminous presence. I cannot give her any signal. My uncle would notice, or one of the many guards on the edge of the room would have a record of it. If I am to fool my uncle, I need to fool Corby too.

So I do not run over to her, or ask her if she is all right. She is alive, and she is not all right. But she will be, just as soon as I get her out of here.

Uncle Mirodag makes some revolting remarks about Corby looking at me. It takes every shred of strength I have to keep my lion from savaging him, right here at the card table.

He'll pay for his disrespect, though. Sooner or later, I will make him eat those vulgar words. Nobody will ever dare to talk like that about Corby again.

The alcohol in my uncle's system is starting to affect his judgment. His eyelids droop as he rearranges the cards in his hand. He holds them close, so I cannot see them. But he is not as vigilant as he usually would be.

Now is my chance.

I take my next card, and pretend for a split second that I'm crushed with disappointment. Then I make my face blank again, as though I've just remembered. I glance up at Uncle Mirodag, allowing just a hint of concern to flutter across my face.

My uncle's mouth turns up slightly at the corners. His eyes shine with glee. From the triumphant angle of his mouth, I'd say he thinks he knows the outcome of this game. And he's sure it will end with me losing.

Let him think it. That's exactly what I want him to believe.

Corby gasps a little when I'm acting out the disappointed face. It pains me that she's going to worry I'm genuinely losing. Nothing I can do about it now. The plan must proceed.

For a second, I wonder if this is worth it. Why am I trying to win back Corby's freedom with tricks? That is not how I want to do it. I want to tear this place apart, take my girl's hand, and take her back home with me.

Yet I cannot risk her life with a reckless act. I

am not armed. Corby's gun is useless. My uncle has firepower, resources, personnel, and sheer ruthlessness on his side. He would wipe us out in a heartbeat. I will never allow that to happen.

Corby Frayne *will* leave this ship safely. I'd kill everyone in the galaxy before I'd let my uncle damage a single hair on her head.

"Oh dear, nephew. Oh dear." Uncle Mirodag is speaking in a sing-song voice, slurring his words a little. Those mauve cocktails must be stronger than I imagined.

"Something wrong, Uncle?"

"I hope your stomach is made of strong stuff. Looks like somebody's going to be doing a little slaying this evening. What is it the writers say? Kill your darlings." He laughs at his own shitty joke.

Corby makes a small, scared sound. I turn to her, holding her gaze for a moment. I must not betray myself, in case Uncle Mirodag's men notice. But I must give her some hope before she slips into despair. We look at one another for a little while, and then she turns away.

There is no way for her to know what I am thinking, without asking directly. And in the same way, her face is as unreadable as I hope mine is. We must wait until later to share our truths.

My uncle throws down one card and picks up another, chortling to himself. If I'm judging this correctly, he's convinced he's winning. Not a chance. This is a game of skill, not luck. I didn't pay enough attention to it when I played with my brother and friends, but this time I'm watching every maneuver.

The stack of cards in the middle of the table topples over. One of my uncle's staff reaches over to straighten it, and I instinctively pull my cards closer so nobody can read them. My uncle looks over, so I frown a little, like I'm concerned at the awfulness of my cards. I'm probably not the world's best actor, but my uncle is hammered. It's good enough.

At last, we reach the final part of the game. All that remains is to lay out our remaining cards and see who wins. I give Corby a lingering look and just hope she can decode it somehow. What I want her to do is stand by, and be alert.

Her limbs seem to tense, and she leans forward like she could get up at any moment. I give my cards one last sorrowful look, and clear my expression back to a blank slate.

"Hey Uncle, did you really want to finish the game now? We could make it best of three?"

I'm taking a chance here, by offering to extend play. I'm doing that because I predict he'll say no, because he looks like he's in a hurry. I'm hoping he'll assume I'm trying to stall because my cards are awful. If he thinks my suggestion is a ploy to string things out, he'll shut it down completely and say no. That's what I want him to do.

"Face it, Jalton. You failed. You are a failure." Uncle Mirodag seems to take a perverse pleasure in saying those words to me. "Your father would be so *proud*. No, wait. The other thing. Your father would be so *ashamed*." He laughs, in a revoltingly oily way.

I say nothing, but just watch him.

"Here we go. Watch and learn, spoiled prince." He lays his cards in one line.

They're pretty good cards. He has a run and he could've won in some games, with some other opponents.

But not with me. Not today.

"Hey, that's not bad. But, uh, my cards are better," I say truthfully, making sure my face says the opposite. "Are you sure you don't want to continue play for just a little longer?"

"Nice try, boy. Show the cards. This game is over."

"You got me," I say, sighing heavily. "Uncle Mirodag, you deserve to see what I have here."

And then I do it. I lay my cards out in an arch shape.

I have the best Kenovian flush I've ever seen. The room falls silent as, one by one, everyone in it realizes the implications of what just happened.

Uncle Mirodag smirks at first, before he sees what the cards are. Then his face drops.

He begins to bluster and rage, but I stand over him, shaking my head. I'm not pretending any more. My fury is real.

"Corby Frayne is coming with me," I say. "Release her at once."

The guards are disconcerted. They look to my uncle for guidance.

"I don't think so," he says, with a dismissive wave of the hand.

"We had a deal," I say, my lion beginning to snarl. I nod at the guard nearest Corby, who unlocks her handcuffs. That's more like it.

Uncle Mirodag stares at me with pure contempt in his eyes. His voice still slurs from all the alcohol he's consumed during the game. "That human is a prisoner. A terrorist. The galaxy is not safe when individuals like that roam free. We are not releasing her, Jalton. It is out of the question."

"Did you know the Imperial Order space army killed her family?" I thunder. "We wiped out millions of Earth people. This regime is rotten to the core, Uncle Mirodag. I think you know more about that than you're admitting."

"Stop trying to distract me from the real issues. You're a loser, Jalton. You can't handle politics any more than you can handle your own life. And you're not taking a terrorist anywhere."

"She is coming with me," I repeat. "You think you're going to stop her leaving? You'll have to go through me first."

And just as my uncle's guards all raise their guns, I shift.

In lion form, I leap at my uncle and shove him over. We crash to the floor.

Jalton has shifted to his lion shape before I can even register what's going on. It takes everyone else by surprise too. One minute, he's standing there with a stormy look on his face. Then suddenly he's a lion.

Would I ever get used to having a friend who turned into a lion every five minutes? I'm not sure. Plus even asking myself the question is stupid. It means I'm ignoring the feeling inside that tells me I want to be more than friends with him.

But Jalton's a *prince*, for crying out loud. If we even make it out of here alive, he's not exactly going to keep in touch. Sure, he has the hots for me, or maybe he likes to try to sleep with every willing woman he meets. Either way, that's not going to be enough to get over our difference in status.

I'm grateful he didn't kill me. I'm super grateful

he helped me with the chip, and is fighting for me right now. That's more than I could have hoped for. It has to be enough.

He springs at his bad uncle Mirodag and roars right in his face. Mirodag lies flat on his back, drunk and useless. It's great to see him that way, after everything he put us through.

But that doesn't last long. When he comes to his senses, he shifts too. Of course he does.

And Mirodag's not a lion. Nope. He's a fricking *dragon*.

The fuck?

"You didn't tell me your uncle was a dragon," I shriek, as I dart out of the way of a jet of fire. Jalton doesn't answer, because he's busy being a damn lion. And also snapping at his uncle's scaly throat.

I look around the room wildly, trying to work out what to do for the best. Is there any way I can grab a weapon? My restraints are gone, since Jalton won the game. But I have a feeling trying to waltz on out of here through the front door isn't going to go down too well.

We need to defeat these bastards. That's the only way we're going to leave in one piece. The way Mirodag's blasting out fireballs, we'll be lucky not to leave in an urn.

I notice one guard is distracted, having a conversation on his earpiece. Who knows who's listening in? But I can use this opportunity. Slowly and carefully, I inch toward him. Nobody seems to notice I'm moving.

"That's correct," the guard is saying. He's trying to hold the conversation privately. That's good. It means he's so busy thinking about keeping his chat on the down-low, he's not thinking about the gun he has so carelessly left in an open holster on his hip. Unluckily for him, I'm pretty good at relieving authority figures of their guns.

Mirodag burns a chair to cinders, and a few guards run over with fire extinguishers. I grab the moment.

Slipping my hand down the side of my leg, I very carefully reach over and ease his gun out of its holster.

The guy shifts his weight from one leg to the other, and I freeze. He still hasn't noticed me standing just behind him. That means he also hasn't noticed I'm now holding his gun. I'm trying to keep to his blind spot, so that even if he turns his head, he won't see me in his side vision.

Mirodag swipes one leathery wing, and Jalton is knocked ten feet across the floor. When Jalton gets back to his feet, he roars so loudly it makes me jump. Man, that roar is loud. I want to plug my ears, but I can't risk drawing attention to myself.

The guard whose gun I stole is still talking. I figure there are enough distractions going on right now, and I should be able to make my move.

With a steady motion, I grip the gun and hold it behind my back. It's a pretty standard issue LazerJet 2b, so I should be able to handle it okay. None of its functions will be too fancy for me to recognize. I mean, it's still a hell of a lot better than my own crappy gun, but that's not difficult. A kid's water pistol could go head to head with my old gun, and it'd probably win.

I wait until the dragon is turned to the side, and Jalton is out of the way. Then I aim for the eye. It'll only work if I hit a vulnerable part, and there are precious few of those on a dragon.

Boom. My borrowed LazerJet hits the dragon right on its scaly cheek.

Aw, shit. That's not going to work. He won't even have felt that. And he's going to be mad as hell when he sees I'm taking potshots at him.

Mirodag turns his mighty head and makes a snarling noise. Puffs of dark gray smoke pop out of his nostrils. He's one badass motherfucker.

Jalton roars again, but Mirodag rears up and extends his wings. The room is big enough for him to go to full extension, but not really enough for him to fly. Luckily for me. I think I'd faint if he divebombed me from an aerial position.

It becomes obvious that Mirodag, the big-ass dragon, is stomping his way toward me. Oh boy.

I hold the gun in front of me with both hands, arms outstretched to their full length. I concentrate on keeping it aimed steadily at Mirodag. It's hard, because my hands are trembling and my palms feel sweaty.

Focus. You can do this.

Jalton leaps on Mirodag's wing and drags it downward with his teeth. Mirodag snarls and puffs black smoke into the air. With one shake of his wing, he dislodges Jalton and knocks him into a table and chairs.

I want to follow Jalton with my eyes and make sure he's okay. But Mirodag has turned his attention back to me know. I know I can't take my gaze off him. If I do, he'll have me at a disadvantage.

I'm just one tiny human, next to this monstrous dragon. What can I do?

This.

As Mirodag reaches me, I throw myself down on the floor underneath his massive body and lie on my back, with his legs either side of me. At point blank range, I shoot the gun right into his soft belly. It's the only part of him that's vulnerable to LazerJet fire, apart from inside his mouth and his eyeballs, and he wasn't about to let me get to those.

Mirodag lets out an almighty cry. It's bloodcurdling and loud. For a moment, I feel like the walls might just fall down around us, destroyed by the wall of sound coming out of this dragon.

He stumbles, and I suddenly realize I'm in danger. If he collapses on me, I'm doomed.

Before I can get myself out of that space between his belly and the floor, I feel myself being dragged along the floor by the hair. I squeal. It hurts like hell.

I slide a few feet across the floor, and then a wet nose turns me over. Jalton the lion picks me up by grabbing the fabric of my onesie in his teeth. He runs with me like that, like he's picking up a lion cub by the scruff of its neck. I shut my eyes and fold my arms across my chest, because the bouncing is too much.

We reach the outside of the building just in time to hear an almighty crash.

Jalton shifts back to man shape, in an instant. Naked man shape, of course. I've never seen such a welcome sight in my life.

"That was my uncle," he says, only mildly out of breath from dragging me out of a building with his jaws. "He must have fallen. Now's our chance to get away."

We run to find our ship, hand in hand. My heart is kicking down my ribcage, but I'm happy. We made it this far. Now all we need to do is get back into open space. Even if the Imperial Order has blacklisted us and we can't land anywhere, we'll just fly somewhere else. We can tackle anything together.

"Now what?" I puff, as we catch a glimpse of the ship a few hundred feet away.

"We fly away, Commander," Jalton says, with a sidelong grin. "Unless you wanted to stay and offer a bandaid to my uncle?"

"Uh no, I'm good. Let's go."

We jump on the ship. The doors are barely closed before we leap on each other and kiss like we'll never stop.

Jalton struggles with the fastenings on my onesie for a moment. Then he growls, and just tears the thing off me. I don't even care. I want to feel his skin on mine, more than anything else in the world right now.

"Autopilot on," he calls out to the ship's computer. "Take us home."

He lifts me up in the air, still kissing me. We're moving, but I can't see where, because our lips can't separate. Not for anything. His warm, firm kiss feels like a lifegiving force. I couldn't walk away from this for all the money in the world. This is the best thing in the world. His kiss, his touch... right now, it is everything.

I feel myself being set down on a counter or something, and turn to see. It's the flight desk. He slides my panties off me with one flick of his mighty hand, and I flinch for a second when the coldness of the flight desk touches the warmth of my skin.

He pushes his body between my legs and kisses me deeper, harder, more insistently. His tongue searches my mouth just as his hand colonises my body, taking every part of me as he wants to. His touch is hypnotic. I crave more.

Then he pulls away from the kiss. I whimper for the loss, because he needs to be kissing me. That is the only logical thing that can happen. It is so right.

He ignores my wordless protest, and instead begins to trail kisses down my body. I can't help draping myself backward, leaning my head on the wall of the ship. My skin crackles and fizzes as his hot kisses turn to little licks and tiny nips.

"You're mine, Corby Frayne," he growls, in his deep gravel voice.

I can't argue with him. Right now, I'd agree to anything he said. Although I have a feeling I'll probably agree even in the cold light of day, without his demanding mouth all over me..

He kisses the top of my thigh, and I gasp. He's so close to me, in such an intimate way. I should feel a little embarrassed.

I'm so not embarrassed. Hell, I want him there, and then some.

He shoves my legs apart, and I already know

what he's going to do. I close my eyes in anticipation. I'm so tense that when his tongue laps at me, I almost scream.

It's too good. I can't stand it.

But I need it. I need him.

He spends just enough time down there for my legs to buckle, so he hitches them over his shoulders. This lifts my hips off the flight desk a little. His hands are there now, squeezing and caressing me everywhere while his talented mouth does what he's so good at.

"Oh... my... God..." And I'm there. It's eyewatering. Mindblowing. I yowl like a real wildcat as I explode into a million pieces. At least, that's what it feels like.

He waits for the shuddering to subside, then he pulls away. I burble something incoherent, and he pulls me up by the waist.

"It's time you received punishment for your crimes, Corby Frayne," he murmurs. His voice is dark chocolate and fire.

"Punishment?" I say, only just able to string words together again.

He stands me up, then flips me around. Grabbing my hair in his fist, he pushes me forwards onto my elbows on the flight desk.

Oh hell yes.

"Forty-one violations, I believe," he says, and I

shiver to think of what's coming next. "Unless you want to protest your innocence."

His hand strokes my ass, and then delivers one stinging slap. I gasp.

"Nope. Guilty as charged," I say, turning to look at him over my shoulder. His hungry stare makes me shiver again. And the size of his hardness makes my jaw drop. Surely that can't be real? But it is. It really is.

"Guilty. Yes. That's what I thought."

Another spank to my bare ass, and I'm smarting. Warmth pools inside me.

"Mmm. I'm a career criminal. Show me who's boss."

Spank. "I'm the boss. Don't forget that."

"Yes sir," I say, in my sassiest voice. "Whatever you say, sir."

That earns me another spank. I'd hoped it would.

"Please sir," I whisper. "I want more."

"More?" His voice is ragged with desire. I know he's drinking in the sight of me, bent over the flight desk with my ass in the air. I feel like I might come again just thinking of what could happen next.

"Yes. *More.*"

He presses his hardness against the back of my legs. "Are you sure?"

"Oh God, yes."

He fumbles for a moment but I don't hear the

rustling of a condom wrapper or anything. But I turn to see him smoothing something over himself. I guess Imperial Order protection is super advanced. Whatever. I just need him now, before I melt into a pool of lust.

He presses himself to me again and I push back against him.

"Now," I beg. "Now."

He doesn't need to be asked again. He grips my hips and pushes a little way inside me, and I yelp. He's huge, and it feels like I can't take him. But he slows way down.

"Are you okay?" He dips his head to my neck and kisses it tenderly.

"Yes," I say. "I think we might have to go easy."

"We have all the time in the world." He strokes me all over, reaching around to gently cup my breasts. Slowly, gradually, he eases himself inside me again. I relax, and take him all.

We start to move again, in perfect synchronization. Before long, he pulls out and I yelp once more in protest.

He spins me around so we're facing one another.

"I need to see your face," he says. "I want to look you right in the eye while you come." And then he lifts me up and slides me down onto him, almost all the way.

He's holding me up in the air, rocking me back

and forth, and it's incredible. He's so big and strong, and he seems to be holding me effortlessly. At one point, he holds me with just one arm, and threads the other through my hair to pull my head to his. We kiss lazily, savoring the feeling, until it just gets too much for me.

I throw my head back and moan, as the waves of bliss cascade out from my core. He responds by pushing in deeper, harder, and holding me still while he reaches his climax. When he hits that spot, he roars just like the lion he is.

We half-collapse together onto the pilot seat, damp with sweat and out of breath. He holds me close, and I rest my head on his solid shoulder.

"I'd like you to meet the rest of my family," he says at last. Just like that, out of nowhere.

"Are they all murderous dragons?"

"Not all. Some are jaywalking pandas." I lift my head to look quizzically at him, and he smiles. "Just kidding. None of them are murderous. Or pandas. Apart from Uncle Mirodag. Who isn't a panda. But is murderous. You know what I mean."

"You're a-dork-able. Of course I know what you mean." I kiss his forehead and rest back on his shoulder. "If I'm nice to your dad, do you think he can get me out of the forty-one traffic violations rap?"

Jalton laughs, and holds me closer still. "I'm pretty sure we can let those slide, Wildcat."

"And not just because you're screwing me?"

"Present continuous tense?"

"Excuse me?"

"Screw-*ing*? Not *screwed*?" He looks triumphant. "That means you're planning to do it again."

"Again? Well, I thought I'd let you recover first," I say, with a theatrical wink. "But any time you're ready to go again, you just tell me."

He grabs my hand and pulls it to his lap. The evidence is right there.

"Oh my," I say. "I'm going to need one hell of a nap when we get home to your planet."

"I'll join you," he says, and kisses the sass right off me.

Corby pours another glass of clear water. "You think Tollajif had time to send a copy of the documents to your account before he was killed?"

I finish my mouthful of space food and shrugc. "I don't see how he could have. There wasn't much time between our meeting him, and finding him dead. Sadly, I think we might not have the evidence we need to really bring the criminal element of the Imperial Order out into the open."

"That's a damn shame." Corby dabs the corner of her mouth with her napkin. "So what are we going to do? If you're sure Mirodag survived the gunfire, he's going to tell your dad a pack of lies. It's his word against ours."

"Unfortunately, yes." I polish off the last mouthful of my food, and set down my eating utensil. "Perhaps we should consider not going home."

"What? But where else would we go?"

"Anywhere. It doesn't matter, so long as we're together."

Corby smiles at my matter-of-fact statement. "Cute. You can't check your account from the ship?"

"No chance of that. The account I used carries the highest level of Imperial Order security. I can only open messages in person, back in the palace."

"So there's no way of knowing if Tollajif got the message across without going to your home planet? And if we get there and we don't have Tollajif's evidence, Mirodag will spin lies about us and we'll need to run for our lives?"

"That's about it, yes."

Corby is silent for a moment. Then she looks up at me, frowning. "You want to just run?"

"I am prepared and willing to do that if you wish it."

"What do you wish, Jalton?"

He takes my hand. "I think we should go home to the palace and check in person. And take our chances. My father my not even believe Mirodag. Even if he does, he will probably allow us time to leave again. It would be most unlike him to take hasty action."

"He sounds nice."

"He is. Admittedly, he's going to be a little

annoyed I'm not marrying his choice of woman, but he'll understand in the end."

I look down at my tattered, dirty fingernails. Yeah. Not quite the princess type. "I don't want to annoy your dad."

"You won't. Just be your authentic adorable self. That's all you ever need to do."

"Okay. That, I can handle."

We curl up together on a wide sofa in back, and Corby dozes off on my chest. My heartbeat must be loud in her ear. I don't know how sensitive human hearing is, however. Perhaps it is only a faint tapping to her. Impossible to know.

I stroke her hair and kiss the top of her head. It is a serious concern to me. We could be heading into terrible danger. If we arrive on my planet after Uncle Mirodag has contacted my father, we will be taking a great risk.

Something must have startled her awake, because she looks up with half-lidded eyes and says "Would my father really believe you? I mean, if you contradicted Mirodag?"

"I'm not sure." I think about my father, imagining his face and his voice. "He always favored Reago, my brother. I was very much the afterthought."

"Reago's older?"

"Yes. And in all ways he is what my father wanted in a son. So if we ever fought, my father always took my brother's side over mine." I inhale deeply and exhale, as memories unfold in my head. "Uncle Mirodag, on the other hand, is his favorite brother."

"Shit."

"Right."

"So we're playing Russian roulette here. We have to decide whether or not to go home to your place, without knowing if it'll be our worst mistake yet."

"Basically, yes."

"But if we run away, we might never know if we could have stopped the corruption."

"That too."

"And there's always an outside chance that Tollajif got the evidence to that secret account of yours."

"It's not impossible. Unlikely, but not impossible."

We're sitting in cozy silence, thinking about this problem, when there's a bleep.

"Incoming transmission from Imperial Order Juvenile Justice Department," announces the ship's computer. We sit up, bleary-eyed and baffled.

The navigation screen suddenly switches to a videocall camera. On it, a man with an eye patch and a cloud of steely-colored hair leans forward.

"Mr. Zonab!" Corby shrieks.

I look at her, then him. She flaps her hands at

me. "Oh, sorry. This is Mr. Zonab. He's my probation officer. You know, from my juvenile
conviction."

I greet this Mr. Zonab.

"How did you know where we were?" Corby
asks. "We're supposed to be--" I squeeze her hand
tightly, to remind her not to talk about anything
confidential. She nods, and her kissable lips close.

"I'm afraid I had to invoke a security clause in
our agreement, Corby." He adjusts his eye patch.

Corby doesn't seem to understand, any more
than I do. "Huh?"

"Usually I stay well back. I only intervene if
there's evidence of a crime. And, as you know, your
retina camera is only on during working hours.
But..." He clears his throat. "When you were
meeting with the Resistance member, it happened
to be during my working day. So I was able to
observe it."

I look at Corby in astonishment. She has a
retina camera?

"Oh shit, Mr. Z. You saw that?"

"Yes." He leans in closer to the camera. "In
strictest confidence, I have much sympathy with
your position." He gives a pointed look, and Corby
claps her hand to her mouth.

"Oh my God, Mr. Zonab? You're a supporter of
the Resistance?" She shrieks with laughter. "You
work for the Imperial Order!"

"We are many." He nods at the camera. "I shall say no more, for I know you have a senior royal in there with you. But from what I saw, he is fairly trustworthy."

"I think he is," she says, squeezing my knee.

"Your Highness, I took the liberty of contacting Tollajif immediately after your meeting, before his tragic demise. He sent a copy of the documents to me as well as to you. The Probation Department has a secure mail system too, you see. It seemed as though it would be a good backup option. You know, in case anything happened to you on the way back."

Corby and I have no words. None at all.

Finally, I manage to speak. "You have a copy of the evidence we need? It is safe?"

"I do. And so do you. When you open your secure account, you will find it there. Tollajif sent them both together. My copy bears your address as well as mine. I assume the reverse is also true."

I grab Corby's hand and kiss it. "You know what this means? My father will have to believe us. We can go home."

Corby smiles brightly. I want to grab her, but now I'm aware the retina camera is on, I'm suddenly thrown.

She reads my mind. "That's awesome. And Mr. Zonab?"

"Yes?"

"Do we really need the retina camera now? I mean, now that I have constant supervision by a senior member of the Imperial Order?" She waggles her eyebrows at Mr. Zonab, who seems to blush.

"Your Highness," he says, in a serious voice. "What are your intentions toward this human female?"

"I intend to make her my princess," I say, immediately.

Corby gasps.

"Do you intend to accept this offer?" he asks Corby.

She says nothing but nods frantically.

"In that case, I release you to Prince Jalton. Your retina camera feed will be deactivated immediately. You may have the lens removed at any time."

"Thanks," Corby says, still looking stunned.

"I wish you both the very best," he says. "Good luck with everything. If you need anything, please shout." He raises a fist and says "Long live the Resistance." Then the screen goes dead.

"Audacious closing comment, considering the audience," Corby says. "Man, I wish I'd known that guy was such a badass. It would've made our annual check-in meetings a whole lot more fun."

"You never did tell me what your juvenile conviction was for," I say, sliding my hand up her leg. "It must've been something severe."

"That's a story for another time," she says, slipping her hand into my jacket. "But first, let's celebrate our freedom."

I kiss her. "To freedom. And to us."

"Us."

✳

As we fly back to my home planet, I'm filled with joy and pride. I cannot wait to introduce her to my family. And I cannot wait to see the look on Reago's face when he realizes he has a shot with Lady Simla after all.

The last few days have turned my world upside down. I can't believe I was reluctant to take on my punishment.

I lost a bet, and won my fated mate.

Guess I'm a pretty lucky prince after all.

"Your husband-to-be awaits you, madam." The personal attendant curtsies deeply, pulling out her skirt on both sides. She's adorable. Apparently, I get to keep her when I'm a princess. I'm going to need to stop her curtsying though, because she's going to put her back into spasm one of these days. Still, it's cute.

I turn around, with great difficulty. There are four wardrobe attendants holding up various parts of my dress. I'm wearing a huge silk number, embroidered with gold thread and embellished with pearls. It's so heavy, I swear I'll just fall backwards onto it if the attendants walk away. Here's hoping they don't leave me.

We somehow wrangle ourselves through the door, and head for the ceremonial hall. Jalton's family palace is unbe-frickin'-lievable. Like really incredible. There's nothing like it on Earth. There was nothing like it even before the Mars war. It makes all the most luxurious buildings on Earth look like mud huts. I'm continually awestruck by the beauty and size of the place.

And Jalton? Man, he's the best. If you'd told me I'd meet my soulmate in a prison cell, and he'd be a royal shapeshifter? Yeah, I'd have thought you were nuts. But here we are.

He's the most amazing man I've ever met. The guy even arranged for my ship's computer Neela to be implanted in one of my brand new serving droids. We can be BFFs forever. It's so sweet.

And even if Jalton weren't a prince, I'd snap him up. Even if he were an enforcer. Seriously, I'm so in love with this dude, he could be a butt-ugly enforcer, and I'd stick around. That's how much I want to be with him.

A swell of heavenly orchestral music rises as I enter the ceremonial hall. Everyone turns to watch me enter, with my attendants.

Jalton turns, and our eyes meet. My heart bangs against my ribs. I smile and well up with tears all at once, like a crazy person.

He looks at me with such love, and I know. I just know.

This was meant to be. We belong together. Fated mates. And I can't wait to spend the rest of my life with this lion of a guy.

My bride enters, and a hush falls across the room. She is here.

She is so beautiful, I can hardly believe my eyes. Not because she looks better in her wedding dress. She looks as beautiful as she always does, in or out of any clothing. Her beauty is devastatingly powerful to me. The more I get the know her, the more I fall under her spell.

She edges down the aisle, slowly because of the great structure of fabric she wears. She carries the traditional Imperial Order gown well. It is more elaborate and heavy than Earth wedding dresses, she tells me. But she was happy to wear it. She says she wishes to be a traditional princess for her wedding day.

I laughed when she said it, because she is hardly the obedient princess type. She is a rebel and does what she wants. That is just one of the things I love about her.

As she walks, one of her attendants trips slightly and her dress hitches up. I stifle a chuckle.

Beneath her sumptuous pearlised gown, she wears her heavy black flight commander boots. Her way of saying "I'm still me under all this, you know".

That's my girl.

My heart feels like it could burst with pride and love.

As she reaches me, I take her hands and kiss her. I don't care if it is not time for that, according to the rules of the ceremony. We are not a couple which observes tradition just for the sake of it. We take the good aspects of the past, and we improve the things which are not so good. Like the way we changed the Imperial Order.

When I presented my father with the evidence against the Imperial Order, his action was swift and decisive. He acted just as I'd hoped he would. He ordered his staff to stop the rot, by any means necessary.

Mirodag was spared execution, as a senior royal. But he was jailed. He has no prospect of ever being released.

My father gave his blessing to our marriage immediately. The Imperial Order would be renewed with our union, he said. Corby won him over from the moment they met. Who would not love her? She is one in a trillion.

She is mine. She will always be mine.

She looks into my eyes, and hers sparkle at me. I lean over to whisper in her ear.

"I can't wait to see what animals our kids can turn into."

The look on her face is priceless.

And then she laughs.

Her laughter is infectious. Soon, the whole hall is laughing, and almost everyone has no idea why.

Life with this woman will bring me everything I was missing. Everything I didn't know I needed.

I'm going to spend every moment making her happy. And when I see that mischievous Wildcat look in her eye, I'll remember just how far we had to travel to find each other. At least we landed side by side in the end.

The wedding vows take too long. I can't wait to get her out of that dress.

"I love you, Princess Corby," I say, as I slip on her royal wedding bangle.

"Come here and say that, Your Highness," she murmurs.

And then we kiss.

IN THE STARS

Thank you for reading! If you enjoyed this book, would you consider taking a moment to leave a review?

To find out more about the In The Stars Romance line and sign up for new release notifications, please visit us here:

http://inthestarsromance.com/

THE MILLION MILES HIGH CLUB

KALIA: I'm an independent career woman. I shoot the bad guys myself, and I fly my own ship. The last thing I have time for is a man. So when the Celestial Mates cherub tells me I'm next on the list for a mate? I laugh.

But then I see him. Seven feet of alien muscle, a face like a movie star and a mouth that could drive a girl wild.

I can't stop staring at the eye candy, but that's all he can ever be. Humans don't date Yolcadians. And I'll be lucky if I even get off this alien ship alive.

SCORVAN: Yolcadian soldiers swear an oath to stay single. So when the captivating human with the black hair crash-lands on my ship, I know I should keep away.

The problem is, I never was very good at following orders.

I'm going to save this beautiful female. And I'm going to make her mine. Even if I have to fight everyone in the galaxy to get to her.

THE MILLION MILES HIGH CLUB is a standalone book set in the Celestial Mates shared world. It contains a kick-ass heroine, a hot alpha male alien, a wild adventure, thrills and spills, steamy love scenes, and a very happy ever after.

ROCKET IN MY POCKET

CRESTA: My day was going pretty well until I was abducted by aliens.

Who am I kidding? Things weren't really going so great. My science career was failing, the Celestial Mates cherub was on my case, and I hadn't had a date in years.

But being taken to a hostile planet to be impregnated with scorpion-bug larvae? That was a whole new level of suck-itude.

Luckily, I got rescued by some hot alien dude in a military uniform. And he's very easy on the eyes, if you know what I mean. Now we're shooting through the stars, trying to find our way back to civilization.

If everyone just stopped trying to kill us, things would be awesome.

HARKUS: This human female is the most beautiful thing I have ever seen. She is a goddess.

If I had to slay every alien in the galaxy to free her, I would. I am willing to destroy entire planets to keep my beloved safe.

But not all fights are fair.

If we make it out of this adventure alive, one thing is certain. We belong together.

And nobody in this universe will tear us apart.

ROCKET IN MY POCKET is a complete standalone sci-fi fantasy romance novel, set in the Celestial Mates shared world. It is a sequel to **THE MILLION MILES HIGH CLUB** starring Kalia's best friend, Cresta.

ABOUT THE AUTHOR

Suki Selborne is a USA Today bestselling author writing urban fantasy, paranormal and sci-fi romance. She loves reading stories full of magic, drama, suspense, action and fun, so those are the kind she writes, too. Suki lives with her husband, kids, and way too many books, in London, England.

Keep in touch!
www.sukiselborne.com/mailing-list
hello@sukiselborne.com

Printed in Poland
by Amazon Fulfillment
Poland Sp. z o.o., Wrocław